MICK MACNEIL

Alien Invasions: The Chronicles

First published by Nosepeople productions 2020

Copyright © 2020 by Mick MacNeil

First edition

This book was professionally typeset on Reedsy.
Find out more at reedsy.com

Dedication

For my long-suffering wife who thinks science fiction and fantasy stories are just plain weird.

Contents

1

Invaded

When those fourteen huge space ships suddenly appeared somewhere between earth and the moon taking up coterminous orbit over the fourteen most politically and financially influential cities in the world, the people of earth released a collective sigh, "at last!"

It was as if they were waiting for it. After all, most had seen the movies and the TV shows about alien arrivals and invasions. This was to them little more than one step removed from the world of fiction.

In actuality, only a few were aware of the arrival and when they found it to be the real thing, there was panic. Of course, the earth governments did exactly what one would expect. They mobilized their armed forces, armed the warheads and scrambled the jet fighters. There was an admirable futility to their preparations.

Any reasonably intelligent earthling knew in his or her heart that anyone able to produce the technology to drop twelve spacecraft, each one the size of a large city, into orbit around earth without any advanced warning would be unconcerned about little flying machines attacking them. Even the best of the earth fighters and the missiles they carried were unable to leave earth's atmosphere. To such powerful allies, these missiles even with nuclear warheads, would seem puny and limited. It would have taken little on the part of those newly arrived space vessels to decimate the earth in a matter of moments. Fortunately for earth, it was not the aliens' intent.

To be sure, there were a few tense moments when a single object ejected from each of the twelve ships, heading for the cities far below. This happened so quickly there was no chance of evacuating the cities. There was barely time to get to the closest basement or subway station. so in each city there were plenty of spectators, most expecting imminent death when these craft, for that's what they were, touched down in an open park or city square. They looked tiny when ejected, but in fact they were around six stories tall and wide enough to fill most of the open area on which they landed.

There was no heat given off in the landing process and despite their size and the speed at which they arrived they caused almost no injury to spectators on the ground. The few injuries, all minor, were among those spectators who were too close and were blown off balance and tossed around by the air these craft displaced as they touched down. After the first few minutes there was nothing but silence and inactivity from the craft. They sat there, their fuselages smooth, seemingly door less, and, to tell the truth, looking quite unthreatening.

The amazing thing was that except for groups of military vehicles surrounding each of them, on orders of the particular government of the nation where they had landed, and some curious gawkers, life seemed to return to normal in short order. "Oobla dee, Oobla dah," as the late great musical group had put it, seemed to be the order of the day. Life went on. Whether this was a tribute to the implacability of the average citizen of earth, or a consequence of something emitted from the space craft, no one really knew for sure. But there it was, "I don't care if aliens have invaded us, its break time and I'll be damned if I give up my double shot latte for that."

What most people didn't know, at the highest echelons of most national governments negotiations were already under way. The aliens were seeking asylum. They would trade their knowledge of technology to all of earth's nations for the right to stay on earth. They also made two statements that seemed at first, curious to the humans, but became outright startling when the ground craft opened their doors and the first new arrivals came forth. The first thing they promised the earth politicians was they wouldn't get in the way and they would confine their activities to the lesser inhabited area of the sea and the sky. Secondly, they informed them that of all the creatures they had encountered in their journeys through space the earthlings had the closest DNA to their species. This was startling because the aliens proved to be almost invisible with what looked to be rudimentary, translucent bodies. Airborne or in the sea, they could barely be seen.

There were immediate benefits to the arrival of the aliens. Once they had made their way into earth's ocean depths and higher into the sky, aircraft and ship accidents where reduced to near zero. For over a generation, the alien presence was indiscernible to the average human, although some might have caught a fleeting sight of a ghostly shadow somewhere overhead, or riding the ocean waves.

Meanwhile earth's scientific and political minds were getting anxious. They had gotten smatterings of alien technology opening many new and fruitful avenues of research, but they had been given little opportunity to investigate the alien space technology or their medical technology until the day a large number of aliens presented themselves at a world leaders meeting at the United Nations.

To the complete surprise of earth's humans,, the aliens that showed up for the meeting were human in form. To be sure, they looked more like futuristic department store manikins, but they acted and spoke much like their fellow earthlings. The aliens explained that they were working on perfecting a way to morph into human looking creatures for face-to-face meetings and scientific interactions. They invited the earth's scientists and engineers, technicians and various specialists to visit their ships, learn what they wished and adapt what they could for use.

By the end of the second century after the alien arrival, the world had changed completely. While nations remained much as they had been in one way, they had made significant adjustments in policy. Any sort of political posturing was meaningless as every nation had the same access to alien developed state of the art armaments and defenses. A human/alien advisory board presided over the entire earth and its solar system. Technological and scientific advances that had been beyond anything humans could have even imagined not so long ago were freely distributed.

While economies were strong, capitalism and profiteering were both greatly reduced. Immigration took on a whole new look as people could be transported anywhere, instantaneously, not just on earth, but to earth's moon and any number of about to be terraformed asteroids and moons, and the most popular of the new worlds, Mars.

All but two of the alien ships had been virtually disassembled and turned into spacious residential communities just beyond earth's outer atmosphere. They were perfect for those who preferred the long view of earth rather than extraterrestrial dust beneath their feet.

Since one could travel to any destination in seconds, by stepping through a doorway, living on Mars or a large asteroid, one of the moons of Jupiter or an open concept home on one of the alien spaceships was no different from living in the old neighborhood. Everything one needed was moments away. Terraforming of near and distant planets, moons and asteroids was just getting under way so the extra-terrestrial communities were still quite small.

New and reconstructed communities were no longer just streets of buildings. Building techniques combined natural elements along with materials that used the earth to provide homey and efficient residences blending neatly with larger buildings, malls offices and workplaces. Greenery and trees abounded. Space for agriculture, domestic animals and wildlife merged comfortably with communities of all sizes. Crime, although not completely eliminated, was drastically reduced and correctional facilities, on the whole, corrected rather than simply incarcerated.

Life extension procedures offered the promise of a good long life for most of humanity. Many people might live as long as one hundred and fifty years without any significant sign of aging. After that, genetic tendencies took over, but as many as one hundred seventy-five years looked like a pretty good possibility for most.

The earth was steadily reverting to the blue and green planet it had once been. The concern about the carbon footprint was long forgotten. Alien/human power sources reduced carbon usage to nil except for some home fireplaces. As alien invasions go, this one was the very best kind to have.

There were no odd-looking aliens to be seen, no xenophobia and no visible ghettos. The only term anyone came up with to offer any disparagement was to call the aliens 'Lucies' referring to the fact they were so translucent as to be invisible. The social and physical changes were so subtle and progressive as to cause very little disruption. Everything just seemed to work out for the better.

Within a generation, the world was far more livable. The aliens were centuries advanced, but human scientists, working together with alien scientists were very effective in bringing earth up to speed, not only in technology, but in every area of study. It was all pretty remarkable.

Even more remarkable were changes among the aliens. They had, as they had promised, found a way to morph into a human looking being. In fact, in less than a century, aliens had developed the ability to assume the shape of humans. More than just looking human enough to pass themselves off as humans, they had been able to include the entire DNA chain into their genetic make-up. They could access these genes at will and change into a true human, then with proper blocking techniques, return to their original form. Eventually the human state became preferred by most Lucies

The process, was originally designed to reinforce comfort levels among humans and aliens when working together. Most of this occurred in political circles, research and technology and especially aboard the two space ships that contained the science of the aliens. The other ships were being remodeled into human habitations. Interestingly, this process, soon shared by all the aliens, morphed far beyond the original intent to the point where human encounters with the aliens in their true form, their 'Lucie' was very rare, replaced almost completely by human to human appearing interaction.

In actuality, the human portion of the DNA chain made the aliens when accessing those genetics not just human appearing, but for all intents and purposes, as human as the original earthlings. Since it was DNA driven, there was no prototype, no basic models that the aliens assumed. The aliens when assuming human form were as random in their genotypes as their fellow earthlings. Some had brown eyes. Some had blue eyes. Some had green or hazel eyes. Some were blonde, some brunette. Some had light skin while others had dark skin. Many were athletic looking assuming the best characteristics of a fit humanity, others, appeared pretty ordinary.

Of course, handicaps and disabilities were greatly reduced to the point of being non-existent thanks to the advancements in medicine, psychology, and human/alien research. The eye glasses and contact lens industry was on the verge of disappearing but then revived with the development of various visual enhancements and protections

2

Frank and Xara

Frank was 6 years old turning seven when the aliens arrived. It had been all the talk of the first-grade class. To be sure it was a progressive school and the students, while young, were exceptionally bright, sons and daughters of scientists, politicians and wealthy academics. Frank's father was a research physicist and his mother a successful author.

Among the first graders in Frank's class, the discussion was amazingly similar to the discussions of adults around the world as they watched and wondered about the first, queasy steps with the invaders from space. Some students felt that the world was on the verge of an all-out war for its survival. Others were certain that they could arrange a peaceful coexistence, while a third group were fascinated by the scientific potential the alien technology offered.

Frank found himself among the latter group although, to be honest, he wasn't quite clear on the topic. It had more to do with his dad having purchased a telescope allowing Frank and his dad to observe the nearest giant spaceship lying over a city not too far way. When, at least as far as the general public was concerned, nothing had happened by the March holidays, Frank's father took the family to the city to see what the locals were hopefully calling the alien landing craft, the Tower of Peace.

Frank was fascinated and curious. He wanted to know more. When the stories of human/alien research groups began to circulate, Frank's father had been taken to one of the ships and shown around a bit. His stories when he returned home were all that young Frank wanted to hear.

Frank decided then and there that he would find his way onto one of those colossal vehicles. His sole desire was to become a scientist and join one of the teams that eventually would be studying and adapting the alien technology for human use. To that end, he ate drank and slept science. He was accepted into one of the most prestigious science programs in one of the world's most prestigious universities.

He proved to be a brilliant student and received his doctorate in a field one might call technological engineering. At an age when most university students were puking their first beers into the local pub toilet, Frank had taken part in a number of research studies at several universities ranging from prestigious, to first rate and absolute best in their area.

Despite his lofty standings among many of his fellow scientists, Frank was not the boldest of people. His shyness and anxiety often prevented him from being treated with the respect he truly deserved. Although he wanted desperately to join one of the research teams working aboard the two completely intact mother ships it was not to be. That is, until the Dean of Science at the absolute best in its area school, received a request regarding who among the students and staff might be the most useful addition from that faculty. Ones with not only the scientific expertise, but also with the best personality to work on a team of humans and aliens.

Originally Frank's name hadn't come up, but as those named early on the list had other interests, Frank moved near the top as far as grade levels and scores were concerned. As a scientist, he was a great candidate. It was his personality that caused them to hesitate in recommending him. However, in the end, he was the best candidate for the position and ultimately would turn out far better than anyone ever expected.

When the Dean called him to his office, Frank was terrified. Although he had no reason to be, his work was exemplary and his co-workers and fellow students spoke very highly of him. Still. Frank always feared the worst. When he got to the dean's reception area, the secretary told him to go right in. Looking for clues in her expression as he passed by her, Frank could find nothing and remained nervous and befuddled as he opened the door and stepped tentatively into the Dean's office. The Dean was at his desk looking down at some papers he held in his hand. He indicated for Frank to sit. Frank sat, barely on the edge of the offered chair and stared nervously at the Dean. Although it was less than a second for the Dean to put down the papers he was reading and look over, it seemed like an eternity to Frank who thought for sure it would be bad news. "How do you feel about working in low gravity conditions?" asked the Dean.

Frank had no idea what that meant, but felt as if the axe was being dropped slowly but surely. "I spent a week on the space station with the Gamma team, sir. It took me a day to adjust, but after that I was OK."

"Have you ever met an alien?"

"Only when one came to lecture us last semester. I wasn't

seated that close, so I really didn't meet him."

"So how do you feel about aliens? Think you could work with them?"

"Work with them? I guess. I know they look like they are not quite finished," this was something he had heard around the University from the few who had spent any time with an alien, "But, they are scientists, I think I would be OK."

"Not quite finished, huh," sniffed a voice from behind him, "well you may be right about that, but believe me, we are working on it."

"Frank," said the Dean, "This is Araganta, or supervisor Treegh. If you accept his offer, he will be your new boss."

Frank turned to look at the clean and detail-less face of Araganta Treegh. It was all so perfect and hence unreal looking, "Offer? Boss?", Frank felt like he was strangling.

He couldn't believe he was being so inarticulate and continued to stare at the smiling and, yes, undetailed face.

"So, you'll take the position," said the alien extending his hand.

"Position?" asked Frank.

"Sorry," said the Dean, "I hadn't quite gotten to that."

"No problem," said Araganta Treegh turning back to Frank, "so would you like to join an interspecies team working aboard Mothership two, as the earth folk call it."

"You got to be kidding, "said Frank.

He was so totally blown away with surprise that for another moment he was speechless. He wanted to shout, "Man, that's all I've ever dreamed of my whole life," but only let out something that sounded like, "SSSSSSS!"

"No humor, here," said Treegh, "Do you want the position or not?"

Forcing himself to calm, Frank's voice was still shaky as he said, "I would love the position, sir."

"Terrific," replied the alien, "How soon can you be ready to go. I'm going back this evening, you could ride with me, or if you prefer you can take the next shuttle in two days."

"I can be ready in an hour," said Frank.

"Great," said Araganta Treegh, "I'll see you at Murphy Field at 7pm."

Frank was still nodding when the alien turned and walked out the door.

"I will pass the information along to your colleagues here if you wish to get packed. Remember you won't likely be back for several years so make sure you have everything you need," the Dean stepped out from behind his desk to shake his hand, "Good luck. Frank, have a great trip and enjoy your new job.'

'Yes, sir, I'll remember sir. Thank you, sir," he turned around and had to stifle a dance step as he went out the door.

Just before seven, the shuttle taxi dropped him off at the extra-terrestrial departures level of Murphy field. It was a small complex with a few humans and aliens seated near Departure gate two. Frank dragged his two bags across the hall to join them. He was sure he had forgotten something but for the life of him he had no idea what. In fact he hadn't. It was a worry he needn't have had, as the shops on the Mothership carried anything, he or any human, or Lucie would ever need.

"Ahh," came a pleasant voice, "There you are Mr. Mahone, ready to go, "Araganta Treegh waved his hand toward two who were clearly aliens, their faces clean and wrinkle free, in uniforms, "One of you get Mr. Mahone's bags and stow them please."

Leaving the others waiting on the benches, Araganta Treegh

indicated Frank to follow the uniformed aliens through the doorway and onto a small, well-appointed lounge that turned out to be the passenger section of this particular space vehicle. Three other clearly human beings shared the lounge. "This is Mr. Mahone," said Araganta Treegh in a loud voice. He will be joining us aboard Rammazka eirn. " Turning to Frank, he explained, "That's what we call Mothership two, I'll let you introduce yourselves over the next twenty minutes as we prepare for departure and make our way to the ship."

Within seconds, the two men and one woman introduced themselves and were engaged in a pleasant conversation about alien technology when Araganta Treegh called to them, "better sit down, we are about to take off."

There was a tiny indefinable change within the passenger lounge, but it was so slight and fleeting one would be hard pressed to put a name to it, or even be certain he had sensed it.

Several minutes later Araganta Treegh stood up from his seat. "Well," he said, here we are."

The passengers followed him through the door and into a spacious reception area, then Treegh waved his hand expressively around him, "Welcome to Rammazka eirn, make yourselves at home."

At first the area seemed deserted except for their small party, then Frank began to notice fleeting glimpses of slight, translucent forms around the area. Some were at little machines around the far end of the space while others seemed to be clustered in small groups or by themselves, hovering just above the human like furniture that was spread throughout.

Following Araganta Treegh Frank accidently bumped into one of the forms that was in the process of changing locations, "sorry," said Frank.

"No problem," returned a disembodied female voice as the form moved away.

"These are our flight control and mechanic team. They are currently on break. They tend to retain our natural form as it is easier to get in and out of where they work. They speak a number of human languages as well as several alien ones. If you have a question, just ask, they will be happy to answer. Oh, and you will find that they are more apparent to you in their translucent form over time."

Frank could hear a quiet disembodied giggle and another female voice, "we're a regular information bureau."

"Sorry, "said Frank.

"Oh, crap, you weren't supposed to hear that," said the voice.

Frank caught sight of a vague form moving quickly away from him.

"This way," said Araganta Treegh as he stepped into a large passageway leading out of one end of the arrival area.

Frank, along with the other new arrivals were given state-rooms similar to his one bedroom apartment on campus, only far better appointed.

"You will be provided with a three-day introduction to life aboard a Rammazka," Treegh informed them, "And then you will be placed with your specific team who will apprise you of your work and then you can get down to what you came here to do,"

The mother ship or Rammazka was an alien city. And the introductory tour showed this clearly. There was everything that you would expect of a city, recreation areas, business areas schools and colleges. There was no police force or military force. There was a small group of unarmed security forces, some in human form others in their original form, whose job it was to redirect the curious away from some areas. Mostly the redirects they dealt with were young and curious. As adults, they would have clearance for virtually every aspect of the ship. Other security officers dealt with humans who might get lost or risk blundering into some part of the ship that might prove dangerous for them.

There were shops and stores with mysterious items on sale. Most were far less mysterious than they looked, for like the natives to this city, they had their own unique forms but worked pretty well the same as the objects found in stores on earth.

A large portion of the ship was made up of scientific and technology labs. A great deal of interactive work was going on analyzing, retrofitting, incorporating and experimenting with a whole range of things developed by these aliens on their own or borrowed and adapted from other alien cultures. There were centuries worth of data and technology to go through and the teams that worked on it represented the greatest minds of two worlds. Frank fit right in.

Over the first few years he gravitated towards the alien who shared most closely his education and knowledge a female alien named Xana with whom he discussed and compared and shared speculation on those aspects of alien science they worked on. Xana assumed a human form to work with Frank and soon he lost sight of her unfinishedness. She had a sense of humor, as well as a vast intelligence and Frank enjoyed working with her. He would go home at the end of the day satisfied with the work he had done and strangely anxious to get back to it.

The beginning of each work day was the same for Frank. He would stop at a kiosk that offered human and alien foodstuffs for the workers in the science and technology section. There he would order a more than passable cup of coffee and a compact alien style meal that combined nutrients similar to an earthly breakfast. Frank had found it particularly tasty and filling. In fact, the bulk of alien food was perfectly edible for humans and any nutrients that might be specific to aliens were either digestible or passed through the human system without effecting it in any dangerous or risky way.

Frank would bring it to his working area and put it down well clear of whatever he was working on. Then, as the early part of the day passed he would take a mouthful or two. The food and the coffee always tasted fresh no matter what. He noticed that Xana was similar to him in that way. She had discovered a liking for coffee and the meals she ate were not only similar to Frank's but often were closer to an earth meal than the traditional alien ones. They laughed about that and often when something in their work seemed to click or suddenly made sense, they would tap coffee cups together and have a drink.

After two years when Xana took two work cycles off without any explanation Frank was nonplussed. He knew better than to ask anyone. An alien's private time was as important to them as private time was to a human. For all Frank knew Xana might belong to a small alien cultural group that celebrated a ritualistic holiday that kept her away for those two work cycles. Needless to say, he was quite surprised to come in to work one day and find a beautiful human girl sitting at Xana's place.

Stepping up to the girl, he could clearly see that there was nothing unfinished about her. She even had some freckles on her cheeks. Still, as uncomfortable as that made him, he couldn't stop himself from saying, " Excuse me, that place has belonged to my partner Xana. Has something happened to her, or are you in the wrong place?"

"Well,' said the pretty young woman, looking him straight in the eye. " I guess that proves it then. The genotyping really does work,"

"I don't know what that means," said a flustered Frank.

" I guess it means I have achieved my human genotype if you don't recognize me. I wanted to surprise you and underwent genotyping to naturalize my human form. I guess it works."

Frank looked completely confused causing the young woman to laugh, "Oh Frank, it's just me, Xana."

"Xana," mumbled Frank.

"Yes," she responded with a laugh, then her face went serious, " you know that since we arrived we have been working to be able to take on human form for meetings and working together. Up until now, the best we could do was take on those somewhat simplistic human forms, but our geneticists have been working to improve on that. One of the reasons we came to earth, apart from its natural beauty, which, I might add, you natives were doing your best to destroy, was because of all the species we encountered you were the closest to us genetically. Your DNA quite closely reflected our own, slightly less complex, but very similar. At first we thought that because you were so similar at a basic genetic level we could blend together because we had so much in common. Imagine our surprise to find you so different in form from us and how diverse a species you were."

She continued to explain how the geneticists had held back their arrival in earth space while they determined how earth people could be so much the same and so very different. They were able to do some gene manipulation that allowed them to morph into human-like creatures but unfortunately lacking in the fine details that caused the earth people to say they were unfinished.

More recently the geneticists figured out the DNA and were

able to replicate natural genotypes among the alien species. Its original intent was for those who would spend their time on earth, working there with politicians and coordinating interspecies relations to fit in better.

"I, however," she timidly added, " did it for you. I like you. We seemed to be getting along quite well, but I thought you would feel more comfortable working alongside someone who looked completely human."

Frank was shy of this new Xana and looked at her from the corner of his eye. She was certainly a knock out. He always believed that someone as beautiful as her was way out of his league. "I,I liked you the way you were. You are so smart and so funny. Being with you was something I looked forward to. I even missed you when you were away for the last two work cycles."

"Well, I'm sorry Frank, the change is permanent, I can't go back."

"No, no," Frank shook his head, "I wouldn't want you to go back...it's just that you are so beautiful. I've always felt anxious around beautiful women."

"Oh Frank, that is so sweet. Let's get back to work. I'm sure we can overcome that."

They did and he did. The qualities Xana had always displayed and had caused him to enjoy his time working with her remained. They still clinked coffee cups to celebrate a success. They spent hours reviewing their work together. Frank would occasionally pause for a moment to look at her and realize that she was the most beautiful woman he had ever seen. Then they were back on the job and she was the same old Xana that he had always known.

He found he was living for the times they were together. It

took him some time to figure out that she felt the same. Actually, she had to tell him, but it became clear that Frank and Xana were in love. They may have loved their work but they loved being together more.

They became inseparable spending work cycle off days together, walking through the Entertainment section taking in musicals and theatre together, riding the high-speed transport to picnic on the observation decks. They had their favorites; one that looked down on the earth, the other that looked out at the moon and the space beyond. But most of the time they spent looking at each other.

Frank sent pictures of he and Xana to his parents and they got very excited. They had always hoped their son would find a nice girl and settle down, perhaps provide some grandchildren. Of course, Frank had neglected to inform them that Xana was an alien. When he finally did, they had some misgivings regarding grandchildren, but they had to admit she looked very much like an earth girl and a very beautiful one at that.

Life on board ship was not quite the same as life on earth. Xana did not know her actual parents, but she had a small community of nurturers, male and female with whom she had grown up. They had some misgivings as well. They were uncertain about an interspecies relationship and the self-nurturing process they might set up with their off spring. No one knew what the consequences of an interspecies relationship might be. But Xana and Frank seemed to be truly in love.

Frank's Parents and some of his friends and relatives who knew him on earth were shuttled to Rammazka eirn along with an old Irish priest who had always wanted to go onto space. He and Superordinate Commander, the captain of the ship and mayor of the city it contained, together blessed the marriage.

19

The wedding was apparently the last private event in the two lovers' lives.

The news spread rapidly among the youth of each species, Social Media had not gone away and had grown popular among the young aliens. Often an aircraft would pass by a nest of translucent youth hanging out, invisible to the naked eye except for their mobile communicators. Many of the young aliens began applying for genotyping and could be found on earth making friends with the humans. Many of the humans were not sure of the differences between themselves and the aliens. Although aliens could revert to their Lucie form. That was, as it turned out, irrelevant as alien youth and human youth proved to be far more alike than different.

Frank and Xana's marriage became a matter of public interest among humans and aliens alike and when the word went out that Xana was pregnant the discussion on social media nearly shut down all other global communication.

Supermarket tabloids and celebrity magazines were filled with stories and speculation about Frank and Xana's soon to be arriving, child. The birth watch was massive and every time Xana went in for an examination or sonograph, work slowed and in some places stopped completely for the duration of Xana's medical visit only reverting to normal after a thorough discussion of what the doctors might have told her.

Paparazzi followed Frank and Xana everywhere, even aboard Rammazka eirn. How some of them got there no one knew? However, it wasn't just the earth population following the progress of Xana's pregnancy, the aliens were just as interested and just as curious. Whenever the two went to work aboard Rammazka eirn, they were followed by Lucies, humans and human genotype aliens.

Frank, remembered what Araganta Treegh had told him when he first came on board the Rammazka, that he would eventually be able to better see the Lucie forms of the aliens the longer he lived among them. It was true, in fact, he often felt like he was stuck in a gigantic bowl of vanilla jelly as he made his way through the crowds to work.

While Xana was still working, the humans and aliens aboard the mother ship seemed to all take their break to come and check out Xana through the lab window. The mixture of people and what Frank saw as huge ice cubes was almost overwhelming. He could detect rudimentary seeming ears, rudimentary seeming mouths and beady eyes that followed Xana wherever she went. He would have liked to bring it to a stop, but he was too shy and too polite to ask the spectators to give them some privacy or the pushy paparazzi to back off. So, when Frank brought Xana to the hospital to have the baby, thousands of communications devices where held up to take their picture/ Alien Lucies floating above the crowds, were also shooting the arrival with their mobile communicators. Video cameras lined the walkway, reporters pressed in asking such questions as, "how do you feel?"

"Are you excited?" "

"Will you be with her in the delivery room?"

"Are you hoping for a boy or a girl?"

And countless more inane questions. Unfortunately, there was clearly no one there to tell the reporters to give themselves a shake and stop asking those stupid questions.

Fortunately, medical emergencies were becoming rarer as no ambulance would have gotten through the crowd that surrounded the hospital that day.

Inside the hospital, anyone who had any medical qualification at all were gowning and making their way to the birthing room observatory. It was so crowded that they had to set up video feeds on large screens in the hallways on all the floors. Patients gathered around them in the wards joined by duty nurses, doctors and technicians. It really was no surprise. History was being made here.

The leadership of both humanity and aliens, politicians, ambassadors all waited expectantly. Most knew that they could very well be looking at the future. They wondered what effect Xana's genotyping would have on the baby. It could be quite significant as it was her genotyping that made this bi-species baby possible. No one, except for Xana and her few and very close-mouthed doctors had any idea of what the child might look like. As the time grew closer speculation became wild. Perhaps the baby would be a translucent human or part Lucie part human, or completely one or the other, or possibly totally different from every one.

When the two tiny beings decided to enter the world, one following the other, they looked to Frank and to everyone else observing like two perfectly normal human beings, one male, one female. No one beyond Xana, Frank and a small group of doctors and medical technicians had known about the twins.

When, after several hours the news was broken millions cheered. Some were a little disappointed at the fact that they appeared to be perfectly normal human babies, but every one embraced them and they were followed closely for the first two years of their lives. By then they were no longer unique as there were more and more 'interspecies offspring' coming into the world. The alien parent was genotyped human and the infants all appeared to be perfectly normal human beings with no apparent alien traits at all.

The new born were named after their grandparents, Frank's mom and dad, and the senior guides of Xana's development community. The boy was named Patrick Gargragz eod Mahone and the girl was Drangiz fere Marianne Mahone. Paddy and Dranny seemed happy enough with their names as they smiled and gurgled contentedly though the combined Christening, and welcoming ritual.

Although relations between Franks family and Xana's development community were awkward to begin with, by the time of the Christening/Welcoming, they had become quite friendly, finding more similarity than difference between them despite the fact that some of the older aliens continued to hold firmly to their Lucie forms. Given their mutual love, interest and affection for the newborn twins, no difference seemed to be too great.

Even Franks stodgy conservative great uncle Charles ended the day of Christening and Welcoming exchanging stories with Superior Guide Gartouth who was one to stubbornly retain his Lucie form. They may not have shared similar looks, but they shared amazingly similar stories and lots of mutual laughter. Here, it seemed, human and alien were becoming more and more bonded, meeting as equals and enjoying each other's presence as friends.

For all intents and purposes Paddy and Dranny were typical tiny humans. It would be a number of years later before the report of Paddy's first small injury became public. He had drifted up from his crib to take a closer look at the mobile that Frank and Xana had placed above him and had got caught briefly in the mobile strings. He was quickly freed with minimum discomfort and little physical injury, but by then, these interesting qualities of bi-species off spring had become well known as more and more bi-species couples discovered these special qualities of their babies and made them known.

They could, to some extent, float and propel themselves through the air like alien adults in their human form. They could make themselves hard to see and they could communicate telepathically with fellow infants, whether bi-species, wholly human or wholly alien. While they would retain some aspects of these abilities into adulthood, they could not communicate telepathically with their parents or other adults of either species who had preceded them, but only within their own generation and, as it turned out, in the generations that followed.

There was an interesting affinity between humans and genotyped aliens and interspecies connections were continuously being made leading to a rapidly increasing bi-species population. Terraforming projects opened up more and more places where humans, aliens and bi-species beings could find a home. Humanity and their alien friends were no longer earth bound. Within generations the process of populating the entire solar system was well under way. Only the sun, formally identified as Sol1, would remained uninhabitable.

The most fascinating thing about all these changes, they had taken little more than a century in earth years to get there. Even more interesting was that the colonies were community centered and within them lived aliens, humans, and bi-species who grew these communities based on mutual interest. Psychological rather than physical factors determined the make-up of these communities.

By this time, most of the aliens had human genotyping and interracial mating was leading to more interesting combinations of bi-species offspring. There were those who were more or less human or alien, some in whom alien blood dominated, and some in whom human blood dominated, but in every case the bloodlines and the capabilities they presented were far less important than their mutual interests, whether scientific, academic or artistic.

The aliens had brought a maturity to humanity.

3

Life on Mars

The earliest extra-terrestrial settlements were the twelve alien mother ships, the Rammazka, along with one on the moon and several on Mars. Between the technology and the terraforming, the new Martian habitations were well protected from the historical geological vagaries of the red planet. In many rifts and valleys, the amount of life giving oxygen and the added warmth brought about by terraforming and the solar reflectors carefully placed around the planet were enough to allow towns to develop there without the synthetic domes in which the earliest colonists had been forced to spend most of their time.

The largest community on Mars at that time, still in the early stages of terraforming had a population of about fifteen thousand. The homes and buildings were in line with the combined human, Lucie building procedures that blended built and natural elements into a tasteful and elegant construct. Although it served as a very effective camouflage, looking like a natural, or in the case of the red planet, a somewhat unnatural landscape due to the greenery terraforming had imposed. At the time we are referring to, terraforming was limited and the browns and reds of Mars predominated, while less so within the rift valleys and craters where terraforming was moving apace. Still, the vast surface of the planet remained unchanged.

Camouflage was the least important reason for the environmental buildings of the combined human and Lucie (now generally referred to by terms such as grampa, pops, mom, auntie or hey, you) construction was primarily about economy. These buildings were easier to heat and cool, easily linked to power and communications grids, grids that were virtually invisible and based on the solar power gatherers that allowed the Rammazka to operate at high efficiency over the millions of light years they had journeyed through space, often many light years from the nearest star.

This community, not so subtly named, New Homestead, was close to the planetary equator. It was contained by two good sized rift valleys and a large crater valley. While this valley had been created by an asteroid strike thousands of years earlier, it didn't hurt to base the building site on the adage that lightening rarely strikes twice and hope it was true of asteroids. By now, however, most of the asteroids were being manipulated into coherent orbits in preparation for terraforming, greatly reducing the already rare possibility of an asteroid strike on Mars.

The air of New Homestead was clean and crisp. The temperature, although colder than would be comfortable for most earthlings and remaining that way all year round, didn't stop the natives from adapting to the point that light jackets, t-shirts and as often as not, short pants were the standard attire for all except the working stiffs, male and female, They tended to share the same uniform, rust colored long pants and turtlenecks with a dark brown jacket.

The citizens of New Homestead were, by and large, a happy bunch although some swore that there was at least one grouch to be found living on every street. Many had made Mars their home for several generations. With the extended lifespan that meant that the Mars settlements were rapidly approaching their 200th year since emigration there had begun in earnest. A large number of the adult population had known no other home. Many had seen earth only in videos despite the fact that low cost wormhole transit doorways could be found nearby that would take them back to earth or to any of the settled colonial communities for a very low cost.

Those who had some Lucie heritage and there were many among the first to emigrate to the Mars colonies were happy to stay put on its natural planetary surface. That was probably the result of a need buried strong and deep in the heritage of a species that had spent a millennium in the artificial world of the Rammazka, the Motherships. For most, humans with and without Lucie blood, the move to a new world was enough for them. The few vagabonds and there were some, primarily with a dominant earth heritage, loved the wormhole gates visiting as many of the new settlements as possible.

Dirk and Mara had some Lucie blood. Mara was the daughter of Paddy and Dranny's younger sister and Dirk shared alien blood through his father who was one quarter Lucie. There was still some notoriety in being part of the original mixed family, something that Dirk and Mara Mahone were intent on escaping when they moved to the newly terraformed Mars.

Life was good for them on Mars. They blended in well becoming part of the community, a small one called Redstone Hills, a suburb of the larger Martian City of Barsoom the capital of New Homestead.. Barsoom was the name 'The Peoples' of Mars in Edgar Rice Burroughs's, John Carter stories had called their home planet.

Redstone Hills was named after the hills that rose above the terraformed community. Redstone Hills was a wonderful pace to raise kids. These new Martians had ample space to ride their bicycles, build their hidden forts and best of all the marginally terraformed upper reaches of the valley had breathable air and was a terrific place to explore. Of all the adventurous young Martians of Redstone Hills, Dirk and Mara's son Paddy was the most adventurous.

As the air improved beyond the valleys and rifts where the residents had made their homes, some natural wildlife had found its way there. These original settlers as part of the terraforming process, while not glamorous creatures and totally earthbound, brought life to the cold and rocky surfaces of Mars. A variety of small lizards, tortoises and other minuscule reptiles could be found near the natural water troughs formed by the warming temperatures across the surface of the planet.

While Paddy's compatriots would remain close to the valley rim, Paddy, in his quest to profile the growing wildlife of the high desert would push further afield with his camera and notebook recording the particulars of the growing wildlife populations. Despite their swiftness, few of these creatures escaped his notice. Having made his wildlife observations on the Martian surface, Paddy would lie back on the cool sand and observe the stars. They were quite visible through the thin planetary atmosphere. By the time he was eighteen earth years old, he had developed a pretty good read of the skies, the stars, and distant planets as well as the not so distant asteroids.

He joined the Extra Planetary Security Corps and became what they called a Spotter. While the bulk of the travel between the earth and its terraformed planets and moons and most local travel was done through wormhole gates, the terraforming corporations, especially among the asteroid belt where a great deal of preparation was being done to form the larger asteroids into habitable space, needed to use space ships. These vessels were especially designed to shape and prepare the rocky planetoids for terraforming, usually on the interior, and to build the connections for the ultimate installation of wormhole gates.

The job of the Spotter was to oversee the security of these projects and protect the intricate terraforming equipment from being damaged by the always threatening smaller asteroids. Some, while no larger than a hockey puck, could be quite destructive. While they might be small, their motion was such that any contact with the metallic surfaces of a crane or drill, or the control array of a working ship could cause irreparable damage, or even maim or kill one of the operators. Despite drone technology, terraforming corporations believed in providing the human touch. The bulk of their technology, especially at the beginning of the terraforming process was directly in the hands of living specialist.

Spotters in the asteroid belt were responsible for the safety of these specialized machine operators and their equally specialized machines. The Spotters in their small, fast and highly maneuverable ships could quickly clear the space around any endangered machine, knocking the larger asteroids off course with cannon fire, or blowing them to bits with an energy gun the Spotters called a Rock Cutter. Paddy was a favorite of the terraforming technicians and crew. He was observant and quick, catching stray asteroids and chunks of space rock long before they got anywhere near the work area.

He was cruising around some of the more distant asteroid terraforming sites when one of the Shifters signaled him. Shifter was the name for the vehicle and the person who operated them. Their job was to circle the exterior of asteroids being terraformed to make sure no major cracks developed in the rock. They would then alert the interior or front edge workers while trying to seal the cracks using a high temperature jet spray and a rock fragment shovel.

Shifters tended to operate on local transmission frequencies as their message was selective of the particular site where they were working. Extra site communications was generally done on a ship to ship basis through a physical connection. The Shifter had a communication arm that would reach out and contact the ship to which it wished to communicate activating a receiver on the other ship.

While all space vehicles carried an inter planetary communication device, they were of the break glass and pull down handle in case of a major emergency type and the protocols were fairly extreme. With all the space construction going on, the chatter over open communicators would be overwhelming so physical ship to ship, while requiring some 'flying' skill, was the best way for a shifter to send a message outside of the workplace frequency.

At the signal of the shifter, Paddy guided his ship towards the smaller vehicle until they were close enough for the shifter to extend its communications arm and make contact with the receiver on Paddy's security ship.

"What's the spread?" asked Paddy.

" Ya know, it's hard to be certain, but when I was coming

around the edge of the 'aster' over there, I think I caught a glimpse of something in the distance sneaking around the site. I only saw it for a second or two and then it was gone, but it sure didn't look like one of ours."

"What do you mean?," asked Paddy.

"It was dark with what looked like fins. It moved fast to avoid being seen. I've never seen nothing like it before," responded the shifter.

"Which way did it go?"

"Outbound, all I could tell."

"No quadrasol or periheichel?" asked Paddy.

The quadrasol and the periheichel were means of determining direction. Quadrasol measure worked best for near space using earth and three stars from the known stars surrounding earth's solar system. It provided two co-ordinates that roughly based on the known heading of a space craft could describe the starting point and offer a track within a widening range to help locate it. The periheichal used the nearest point of the Milky way galaxy from earth that through some obscure mathematical formula could virtually pinpoint a space craft or any other object's location in the void between the arms of the galaxy and was apparently adaptable to any other galaxy. Neither Paddy nor the shifter had a real understanding of the math, but knowledge of the basic theory was a requirement for all pilots and crew members before soloing in an extraterrestrial vehicle.

"Maybe Q 187 by 235, " said the shifter, "or something like that."

"If it hasn't gotten too far, I might be able to track it down. Thanks," said Paddy as he pulled his ship free of the shifter's communication arm and began to move deeper into the asteroid field.

4

Tracking

A s he proceeded through the asteroid field in the direction the shifter had given, he began to see in the smaller rocks, the formation of a wake. The shifter wasn't wrong. There certainly was something moving quickly away from the terraforming activity. While the ship he was piloting was designed to withstand the impact of the smaller stones and rock fragments that gathered in the gaps between the larger asteroids, Paddy turned on his HUB allowing him to see beyond the immediate presence of stones and rock fragments.

Sure enough, he could detect a fast moving shape in the distance. It was too far ahead and moving too fast for a visual read, but Paddy was able to register a digital electronic image. There was nothing that Paddy knew that looked anything like this. He "broke the glass and pulled down." Almost immediately Mars Space authority responded to the automatically sent signal.

"What is it, Security P 7niner?" came the digitized reply.

"Located a bogie beyond Terra Ten. Sending digital and visual details, please advise." Signaled Paddy.

"Analyzing data," came the reply, "maintain pursuit. See if you can get a better image."

"Will do," responded Paddy.

Traversing the asteroid field at any speed was pretty harrowing. The speed Paddy had to step it up to, to gain any ground on the unknown ship was downright terrifying. Paddy's ship with its sensors and its connection with Paddy's field of vision could instantly react to avoid the larger asteroids and space boulders, but there was always the risk that the ship would jog around a larger object in its path only to run into a slightly smaller one that hadn't been detected. The asteroid field was no place for a joy ride.

Although he did make some gains on the ship he was pursuing, the particulate of the asteroid field prevented him from getting a visually clear view of the unknown craft, The electronic sensors, however, were able to transmit a more precise digital image back to Mars.

The Mars Space Authority was relaying Paddy's visual images and digital read outs back to the Moon based super library and on to the attached System Security Agency. The virtual computer, a construct dug deep into the lunar surface contained all the data gathered by the Lucies in their travels through space as well as that gathered by the original earth before the arrival, and everything that had been cooperatively gathered since then.

As Paddy continued his pursuit of the unidentified craft, the analysis of the visual and digital details of the craft was carried out. It was soon 90 percent confirmed that it was a kind of scout ship of a species the Lucie's had encountered several centuries back on a couple of star systems they had come across on their route through the galaxy. That species, identified by the data already available were called the Vergazan. This was as close to human language as they could get with the real name of those aliens.

They were determined to be a very aggressive and impulsive species. They had just been on the cusp of developing interstellar travel when the Lucies encountered them. Then, the speed and distance these interstellar vehicles were able to cover was limited. At the time the Lucie's observed them, they had already basically decimated all the planets in their home solar system through misuse of living space and unrestricted cultivation of natural resources. They were in the process of doing the very same thing to the solar system nearest to their home system. The Lucie's determined that this was an exceptionally dangerous species that would most likely self-destruct unless they could expand their interstellar travel abilities, with bigger and better ships and enough communal focus to avoid species self-annihilation.

The conclusion of current data analysis determined that the latter was what had occurred. The analytical data posited an 80 percent chance that the genetically most ruthless and intelligent of the species survived. There was a 95 percent chance that they were seeking out new worlds to exploit and a 90 percent chance based on the likelihood that the small ship represented a scouting and information gathering vehicle that earth was a potential planet to exploit on their destructive route across the galaxy. The data also estimated that there was a window of between 40 to 60 years before any large assault force would break out of the distant arm of the galaxy and another ten years before it would come within range of earth's system.

The only information sent back to Paddy was to continue

pursuit but remain outside scanner distance so as not to be seen. As the unknown craft left the asteroid belt, Paddy held back briefly before leaving the field. He did this to stay out of view of any scanner the unknown might have. If it had a scanner with the range to detect Paddy, it didn't show it and continued on its way out past the gas planets while staying well clear of any ground radar from any of their moons.

Although Paddy's spotter ship had very small sleeping and washroom facilities and limited food supply being mainly designed for local and near local activity, Paddy spent over a week trailing the unknown ship past Pluto and Charon into the edge of deep space before breaking off.

He was then asked by Space Authority to retrace the path back to the asteroid field to see if the mystery ship had made landfall anywhere. Stopping off briefly at Titan, one of the few gas giant moons to have a settlement with a wormhole gate, to restock, Paddy continued his backtracking into the asteroid field.

As he searched the more familiar asteroid belt, Paddy was beginning to think that it was a pointless venture. He was deep in a region of the asteroid belt that wasn't scheduled for terraforming for at least a century when his scanner detected the presence of synthetic material nearby. It might just be a piece of space junk that had drifted out there, but it could be something not quite so innocent given the unknown scout craft he had been following.

Moving closer, Paddy's scanners picked up a larger asteroid that showed a natural formation merged with synthetic material. He proceeded no closer, but signaled Space Authority of what he had found and its location. Space Authority asked him to hold his position until they could send out Science and

Security ships to investigate. Within several hours, two much larger ships pulled up on each side of him. He was asked to come aboard the one on his left for a debriefing.

Slipping his ship into an open dock beside two other Spotter ships, his air lock connected immediately to the larger ship. He was met at the door by a trooper who brought him into a room surrounded by video screens and computer readouts. There was a small table with cushioned benches around it. The trooper asked Paddy to sit and so he did.

Moments later the Space Authority Commander came in. He was a full blooded Lucie, but Geno-typed human. He told Paddy that he had known his grandparents while adjutant on the Rammazka eirn. He had been at their wedding and was one of the guests at the twins christening. He asked how they all were. "Grampa is getting on, but the others are doing alright, thanks," Paddy replied.

After that it was all business as Paddy outlined what he had done since he first communicated with the terraforming company shifter who had initially spotted the unknown craft. After he had satisfied them with all the information regarding his sighting and tracking of the bogey and his retrace and search back in the asteroid field, the commander suggested that he return to his home base, he had done more than enough. He promised he would let Paddy know what he found as soon as he was permitted.

Paddy was back in his Spotter and shortly after landed at Mars Security base. While the ground crew took his ship into the hanger bay to check it out, he went into the officer's quarters, showered and got into his civilian clothes. Not much later, he was in his car heading to his parents' house. Being under no secrecy restraints and there were very few among the system wide society, he could hardly wait to regale his family with the story of his adventure.

5

Marianne

Marianne had just turned nine the day her oldest brother Paddy came home and told them all about the unknown ship he had followed to the edge of deep space. She was especially fascinated by the discovery of the secret alien espionage base hidden in the asteroid field not so very far away from their Martian home in this age of terraforming and settlement throughout the solar system.

Despite the fact that she had among grandparents some who were extra-terrestrial, Marianne and most citizens of earth's solar system, whether they lived on Mars, or a terraformed Venus, or one of the terraformed moons of Saturn or a hollowed out asteroid, thought of themselves as natives. The Lucie presence and Lucie blood was an intricate part of humanity. Marianne, like most others within earth's system, wanted to make sure they were never threatened by hostile extra-terrestrials. This spy base deep in human territory was cause for concern.

From the moment she had heard Paddy's stories, she had decided that she would be a security spotter for the Space

Authority. As her older brother had before her, shortly after turning eighteen, Marianne had joined what was now called the Mars and Extra Planetary Provinces Security Force. In short order she became an MESF ace pilot and on numerous occasions had visited the alien espionage site providing aerial support for the ground troops who guarded the two aliens in their cryogenic sleep, a sleep that SolSytem Security carefully maintained.

Marianne's exceptional flying skill and her knowledge and awareness of the outer region of the system and the alien threat got her promoted to Flight Commander, the youngest person ever, and attached to SolSys Security. She was given command of a flight of five deep space cruisers each with a crew of four humans and one mobile cyborg for navigation and emergency support.

Marianne's flight was assigned to the Neptune, Uranus, Pluto corridors to watch over the terraforming and solar wormholes that would bring light and heat to these distant planets and their habitable moons. Based out of Charon, the flight was also assigned to watch for alien intrusion. The flight flew their security runs for six sidereal months then rotated back to earth for six more with four months furlough.

Often she would meet Paddy, either near earth or outwards of Neptune as he was doing spotting for the larger solar wormholes being put in place. He was essentially travelling back and forth through them also on the lookout for alien intrusion as these wormholes could provide quick transit for near deep space to the inner planets. Should threatening extra-terrestrials appear, it was the job of the wormhole spotters to quickly lock down the wormholes allowing enough heat and light to provide limited functionality on the terraformed outer planetary systems while the SolSyS ships would hold them off long enough for this to be done.

Marianne's team spent much of its time patrolling the quadrant where Paddy had followed the alien scout before it headed off into deep space. Command felt that this would be the likely point of entry for any scout ship as well as for a major assault.

The deep space entry corridor bounded by Pluto and its less visible moon Charon was a dreadfully dreary place to be stationed. Charon base was little more than a hole in the ground heated and lit by one very small solar wormhole. There was a second small wormhole passage to the other planets, but was not easy to use. It was maintained for military purpose and required special permission from both ends to travel any distance.

Except for the wormhole transit to Pluto there was really no place for the SolSys crews to go for R and R. Pluto was more pleasant than Charon. It had a large mall and entertainment center. Beside the main military base there were some residential areas that were generally inhabited by SolSys members on long term rotation. There were very few permanent residences, still the environment was far homier than Charon. This mattered little as the SolSys crews under team Flight Commander Marianne's command were on standby for the entire period of the six month sidereal year of their tour. They stayed close to their ships on Charon most of the time.

What made this bearable for the team was the knowledge that they would be the first to face off against what could well be hostile aliens. The team members while on their four month furlough, although they welcomed it, would begin to get anxious to be back on Charon and take up the watch for the potential invaders.

The best part of the furlough was the amazing work that was done on the cruisers they flew. The armament, the living space, and especially the Overlight Drive were all better each time they came back to them. They carried leading edge weaponry, were fitted out for deep space travel and were significantly faster. The original Vergazan deep space ship that Paddy observed was small and relatively fast. It was equipped with a superlight drive that would allow it to travel the empty space between the galactic arms to the nearest set of stars in about a year.

From the schematics the Pluto sensors and others they could deduce that the Vergazan scout was a fairly cramped two passenger ship that sacrificed comfort for speed. It would be a rough sidereal year long trip for those on board. The new Overlight Drive on FC Marianne Mahone's team's cruisers was able to warp space making the trip across deep space to the nearest stars in a matter of days. The Drive was not weight dependent eliminating the need to strip down the ships for extra-stellar travel. Marianne's team was ready to make that jump on short notice.

Waiting on the Vergazan was tedious. The only time the Flight Commander and her team were really happy was when they were testing the limits of their ships. They had found a field of rocks out beyond the planetary range and would practice snapping out of Overlight and quickly orient themselves into attack mode blasting the rocks into dust. They were good and they were quick. Despite the efficiency they showed in practice, they knew it was not the real thing. They were as prepared for a hostile encounter as they could be, but there had been no wars on earth for centuries. The Lucie's had brought peace and with their mothership space communities, and the terraformed planets, asteroids and moons, there was plenty of room for expansion without needing to confront another group.

The Lucie's, too, brought a calmness to humanity. They had spent centuries in their mother ships learning to cooperate for the good of the entire community. It was essential to the survival of their species and was in their blood, so to speak. As they began to mix with the humans of earth, this attitude of cooperation and need to protect their species became an essential part of the psyche of the natives of earth whether of mixed blood or not. With shared medical technology, biologically based medications, and transfusions there were very few natives of earth who didn't have some trace of Lucie blood.

Now they had to prepare for battle. something to which they were instinctively opposed. This was necessary to protect the species The attitude towards violent defensive posturing was as deeply ingrained in the human/Lucie psyche as much as the bi-species were repelled by the idea of going to war. Because of this, the defenders of earth would not hesitate to meet the aggressive Vergazan in combat and do whatever it took to eliminate any possible threat to their solar system.

Throughout the system preparations for invasion were being made. Battle cruisers with the most up to date technology were in the process of being developed while future crews were being trained in simulators. Minds long trained to make a better and more peaceful world were now planning and producing weaponry. The science of warfare as it had never been seen before was progressing apace.

Flight Commander Mahone and her team were at the leading

edge of these preparations. Their mission was to track any alien ship they detected across open space, following it until it got close to its home, or staging worlds. There they would gather intelligence on the potential threat and assess the possible timeline for invasion and then return back with all the information they could gather about the Vergazan threat. This could only happen with the coming of a Vergazan spy ship into the solar system.

6

Deep Space and Beyond

I t became a very long wait for the Vergazan ship. That was
good news for the developing defense system but not for
the nerves of Flight Commander Marianne's team. Being
in a constant state of anticipation was wearing. After several
years, team members were being recalled to join the command
staff of the battle cruisers. Others retired. Marianne's tour
was nearing its end when one of the deep space sensors set
out around the entrance corridor to the solar system chirped.
It could have been a space rock. That had happened before,
but when the second and third sensor chirped, the time and
direction were revealed to be specific and intentional unlike
the randomness of a space rock.

On the third chirp, Pluto and the inhabited moons of the
outer planets went dark. Charon, hidden behind Pluto, reduced
to minimum operation and the five ships of Marianne's team
were launched and were set to silent running. Tapping into
the deep space sensors, the flight stayed a good distance away
from the path of the Unidentified craft. As of yet they had
not confirmed that it was Vergazan. That would happen when

it went past Pluto, and Charon could make the identification. Until the affirmative tone came from Charon, the team would hang back, hopefully out of sensor scan of the UFO waiting for it to be identified.

To the crews of Marianne's flight, the wait was interminable, then there it was, the tone. Flashing into Overlight warp, the ships went to their stations, Marianne's ship closest to the asteroid field, the others spread out in pre-planned sites among the outer planets including one hidden between Pluto and Charon.

As far as any extra stellar alien could tell entering the planetary system its civilization was barely interplanetary. While earth would seem most populated there was some sign of related habitation as far out as Mars and some of the larger asteroids, most in the early stages of terraforming. Beyond that was silence.

Meanwhile, the Vergazan spies in their tiny asteroid home were waking up to meet their replacements. They were totally unaware they had been under surveillance, kept in stasis for years and fed false information they would believe they had actually observed over the years that had passed since they arrived.

They would return to their superiors to report on the slow development of the planetary civilization that was primarily centered on the planet many referred to as Earth. To the Vergazan hierarchy, the system would appear ripe for the picking and offer little resistance to their own far more developed capabilities.

There was little exchange between the incoming and outgoing Vergazan observers. The former hastened to begin their observations while the latter seemed to be in a rush to get back to their superiors with the information gathered. The outgoing alien ship had barely launched when the tracking process that would follow it to its home base was underway. Inside the observation post the two alien observers were being put into stasis through the modifications to the Vergazan observatory put in place previously by SolSys agents.

As the Vergazan ship made its way towards the deep space passage to the nearer solar systems where somewhere among them their superiors waited, the five ships of Flight Commander Marianne Mahone's command slipped one by one into a path behind them. Remaining at the fringe of their sensors, they were rightfully confident that the stripped down alien ship would not detect them. While the aliens saw their ship as blisteringly fast, it was difficult for the pursuit cruisers to hold back and not overrun them. A voyage that the SolSys ships could have made in little more than a week would take them over a sidereal year at the limited speed they were obliged to use to track the alien's path.

The Solsys cruisers had retained a tight formation until they passed the last deep space sensor then spread out into a wide formation. That way they could make the best use of the extended time their pursuit of the alien would take. They passed the time patterning and sending back projections of the Vergazan ship's possible destination and because they were in unfamiliar and unexplored territory, they ran sensor searches for large rocks and stray planets as well as useful elements or gas clouds, unassumed wormholes and the like. They mapped the corridor, a broad spectrum of the space through which they travelled. As they proceeded they were able to project any dangerous potential or expected incursion of larger objects and gas clouds into the flight path and transmitted them back to Mars for future reference.

This area of space, they discovered, was remarkably free of large potential obstructions. It was, in fact, a clear interstellar pathway suggesting why the Vergazan had chosen it. Their light plus drive could safely travel this particular route to earth's solar system without natural impedance. While physical obstacles were no problem for SolSys ships equipped with Overlight warping drive except at induction and possibly at drop out. There was little risk of this as onboard sensors gave plenty of advanced warning of physical obstacles during reduction from Overlight.

Without the warping factor, high speed impact with a large physical obstacle could do horrendous destruction to a ship, most likely destroying it completely along with its crew. Clear pathways through open space were essential for invasionary forces such as the Vergazan who counted on their speed and the element of surprise for assuring success. If these were offspring of the Vergazan that were recorded in the Lucie files, then they were more likely given to the hammer approach than subtlety in their planetary take overs. Planetary life meant nothing to them. They might preserve a few technical and scientific sites where they could find something novel to aid them, but otherwise they would be there for the natural resources of the planet and a temporary home for their fellows.

As the Commander's flight approached the influence of the stellar cluster towards which the alien was going, they resumed a tight formation. Several hours later as they approached one of the outer planets, their wide range sensor beeped a warning. Another ship had been detected.

What they saw from Marianne's ship's sensors was a craft with a very different configuration than the Vergazan ship. It was cumbersome in design suggesting a merchant or multi-purpose rather than a military ship. The viewers could tell that it had sighted the Vergazan craft and was trying to quickly move away.

Then, to the surprise of the SolSys crews, the Vergazan ship veered off in pursuit of the unidentified craft. The unidentified ship began to navigate what appeared to be a random evasive flight pattern as the Vergazan neared it. Even more surprising to Marianne and her crew, the two ships began to exchange fire. The Vergazan was clearly the superior war vehicle and in short order, the unidentified ship ceased firing and slowed to a stop, Flames gutting out from it on winds of life support air escaping through the disrupted outer skin. The Vergazan turned away to resume its flight path.

For Marianne and her crew this was a clear indication of the viciousness of the Vergazan, that they would break off from their main mission and go well out of their way to take down an unidentified vessel.

7

Alien Allies

The unidentified ship was clearly in distress and from the sight of the enflamed escaping air suggested a slow and painful death for any survivors. Marianne ordered three of the ships in her command to continue the pursuit of the Vergazan while she and another ship went to the aid of the stricken unidentified craft.

As she approached the wounded craft, Marianne and her crew could see from the damage the Vergazan vessel had inflicted on it, just how cruel those creatures were. The stricken alien ship was not destroyed, but rather, terminally damaged. The Vergazan had carefully destroyed the propulsion system and opened breaches towards the rear of the ship, the most difficult area of any ship to access for repair.

Some sort of incendiary weapon had been launched into the puncture gaps igniting the escaping oxygen and likely making it virtually impossible for anyone aboard to get access to the damaged area from inside and reduce the likelihood of any extravehicular attempt to stem the loss of life support. The ship, itself, was clearly inferior to the Vergazan vessel, slower, minimally armed and not designed for extrastellar travel.

I was clear that boarding would be difficult as the Vergazan had made a point to damage all apparent entry ways. This was nothing more than cold-blooded murder. Unless someone from Marianne's ships could get in, those aboard the ship were doomed to a slow and difficult death.

Marianne had the command ship pull up as close as possible to the wounded ship, while avoiding the risk of contacting the incendiary chemical that could clearly burn intensely in the vacuum of space. Using sensors, they found the most spacious area for entry and extended their engagement tunnel out to seal against the side of the other craft. The engagement tunnel used a variation of the wormhole technology that made the trip from one end of the solar system to the other little more than a short walk and carried solar heat and light to the distant lunar colonies of the outer planets. From the tunnel, the wormhole technology would let them step aboard the damaged ship without adding further damage to the hull.

Since the ship was alien and unknown to them, Marianne and her boarding crew donned full extra vehicular attire, prepared to face any sort of complication. Although the sensors indicated an air quality and temperature within the range of human bearability, it could not guarantee it, nor could it guarantee the sort of reception the boarding party might encounter. The crew in the death throes of their ship would not be too happy to meet up with possible adversaries.

The rescue crew needed to board the floundering ship fully prepared for any environment and any reaction. As Marianne and two of her crew made their way through the engagement tunnel, they adjusted their translators, hoping beyond hope that they were universal and that the basis of the ship board aliens' language was available to them.

The Lucies, in their travel through the cosmos, had encountered many different languages. While it was quite likely that those on the ship could speak one of these, or a variant of it, there was still the possibility that they didn't. If that was the case, then the translator may take a long and unacceptable amount of time to understand the alien language, or if it was too different from the languages on file, it might never get it. So far there had been no distress call form the ship, no verbal communication to help the translators.

The three SolSys agents stepped through the engagement tunnel portal and into the alien ship, arms presented, in the hopes any aboard would recognize that they were not arriving with hostile intent. Inside, they could see very little before turning on their helmet lights. With the lights on they immediately realized that who or whatever manned this ship were completely unprepared for the Vergazan attack. Nothing had been secured in anticipation of an assault. Items that looked like food preparation devices or game pieces and a whole array of other less recognizable items, many showing signs of breakage covered the floor or floated aimlessly in the reduced and unstable gravity. A body lay crumpled beneath a chair that seemed to be fronting a control panel.

As Marianne took a step closer for a better look, a light flashed on her from the other side of the control console and a loud voice spoke in an alien language. It took a couple of seconds, but the universal translators clicked in. This was a variation of a known language and it told Marianne and her crew that they better not move any closer if they valued their untranslatable alien (also untranslatable, likely expletives) lives.

Marianne bent down and put her weapon on the floor,

signaling the others to follow suit. "We are not your enemy," said Marianne as the translator instantly sent the message in the alien tongue, "We have come to offer assistance. I am Commander Marianne Mahone of the Sol One solar system security force. My team and I observed the unexpected and unnecessary attack on your vessel by a ship we were following,"

"I know nothing of a Sol One security force, or a Sol One for that matter," returned the voice from behind the control console.

"I'm not surprised," said Marianne, "as we are the first ships from Sol One to cross the deep space between our wing of the galaxy and yours."

"You have come across light years of open space in pursuit of the "Ferkasan" scout ship?" came the voice from behind the console. "Why would you do that?"

"The beings you call Ferkasan have been spying on us and observing our development for quite a long time," replied Marianne, "and we suspect they are amassing a fleet of long range interstellar ships somewhere around here with the plan of invading us."

"Yes, this seems to be the way of the "Ferkasan". They came to our star systems a long time ago. They came prepared to do battle and for an age we fought. Eventually we could fight no more. We took as many as we could and set up refuge colonies on a number of obscure moons from which we tried to carry on the fight. Given our situation, our technological advances were limited while the Ferkasan grew more powerful, their science continuing to advance...advanced at the expense of our home worlds. They have torn every useful element from the earth and befouled the air with their hideous factories."

He went on to tell of the almost total devastation of both

the habitable and uninhabitable planets in their combined systems. It would be vast amounts of time after the Vergazan left before they could return home and then they would find only diminished and crippled worlds.

Coming out from behind the console, Marianne and her crew could see that although nearly as tall as they were, he was otherwise a thin, vaguely mammalian creature. His features were only remotely like humans, two eyes higher on the face than conventional for humans and, for that matter Vergazan, were large and multifaceted. There were no ears but a ring of pointed furless appendages surrounded the top of the head. The mouth was little more than a slit in the center of a grey-blue face that tapered down to the thin body. He had two arms with six delicate looking fingers. The rest of his body was covered in a uniform. Intricate markings on the upper part of his uniform suggested a person of some rank.

He set his weapon, a cone shaped device, down on the control console and attempted to take a step towards Marianne, only to stumble and fall to the ground. Only then did Marianne and her crew notice the dark liquid stain on the leg of his uniform and a rip in it from above the knee type joint to the ankle area.

Although he had fallen, he remained controlled. "Where is your medic?" asked Marianne as she dropped to her knees beside him.

"Unfortunately," replied the wounded alien pointing to the one crumpled at the base of the chair beside the control panel, "that's our medic."

One of Marianne's team members went over for a closer look. He found a large wound on the side of the crumpled alien's head dripping a dark gel like fluid that he assumed to be blood. He passed this information on to his commander and the fallen alien. "I don't know this being's physiology but there is no activity here. He is either seriously physically compromised or dead," he told Marianne who passed the information on to the wounded alien.

"Likely dead," he responded, "severe trauma to the head usually results in death in our species."

"Ours' too," said Marianne.

"There should be a box with wrappings and some pain reducing unguents behind his chair. If you bring it to me, I'll show you how to use them."

Both Marianne and the wounded alien understood the risk in using the medications of another species. They would have to trust the alien's own treatments. Marianne was opening the box her crewman had brought to her when a third alien appeared at a doorway that led towards the rear of the ship. "Karidanz, "she exclaimed along with a sharp intake of air,

"Relax, Zaripeh" said the alien from the floor, "they have not harmed me, but are trying to help. Perhaps you could come over here and help them. My leg is pretty badly damaged."

"Yes sir!" the alien at the door placed her left arm in front of her face and pushed out toward the one she called Karidanz.

Then she was beside him and Marianne, gently moving the torn fabric of the uniform to reveal a badly mangled leg. She poured the contents of a couple of gel packs onto the area where the skin was broken and began to wrap a bandage of sorts around it. The wounded alien inhaled sharply, his hands shaking as she wound the bandage. With the leg bandaged and the unguents rapidly cutting the pain he turned to his attendant. "help me up, Zaripeh."

"Sir" responded Zaripeh, or the Zaripeh, Marianne wasn't sure if it was a title or a name.

Once again the alien placed her left arm over its eyes and pushed its arm out toward its fallen comrade.

"Zaripeh, please, this is not an "alien expletive" parade square, just help me up. New ones..." the wounded alien said to Marianne assuming she would understand exactly what he meant. Having encountered recruits in the past, she got the picture.

"I'm sorry, "he said suddenly, "I haven't introduced myself, I am Karidanz Opper, Commander of this ship and senior adjutant to the supreme commander of this sector. The Zaripeh is Outha. She is what we call female and is also offspring of my offspring. We are very understaffed in this sector, so a beginner and a grizzled old officer like myself are called on to man these ships."

"I am Squadron Commander Marianne Mahone of the Sol One System Security Force and these are my fellow officers Line Captain Guire and Flight officer Kanje. Is this your crew? As she waved her hand to indicate the fallen medic and the cadet holding the Karidanz so he could stand.

"No, we carry a crew of eight."

"Sir, " said the Zaripeh, Cozis Twanna is dead, Cozis Mwyb is badly injured as is Zapeth Jadre. Debriz Yarbe and Under Cozis Hyambuh have gone to the rear of the ship to try and prevent the Ferkasan flame chemical from breaking down the rear bulwark."

"Has a distress signal been sent?" asked the Karidanz.

"No sir," the Zaripeh was uncomfortable.

"Then help me get to the console so I can lean against it and get it sent. You have no problem with that Flight Commander," he asked Marianne.

"Not at all," she replied, and turning to the Zaripeh she said, "dispatch the distress call and then we can check out your wounded and perhaps help your fellows with the bulwark."

The Karidanz , his ship and crew stabilized and the rescue ship not far off Marianne and her crew members were ready to leave. "I would say," said Marianne to the Karidanz, "that in effect, you are hopelessly lacking in comparable ordinance to the Vergazan."

"An understatement," replied the Karidanz, "we are virtually defenseless, our only tactic is to find a good hiding place."

"It would be to our advantage to have a well-armed ally in this part of the galaxy. I will be returning to our solar system very soon. I will present the case to provide you with armament and technology to increase your ships' speed and mobility. I cannot speak for Master Command, but give us one set of coordinates that you can monitor and if there is a positive response, we can meet there. When? That I cannot say, but most likely sooner than later"

She saluted him and he returned it with the same gesture the Zarpeh had used, the arm across the face, palm spread and the arm and hand then pushed out towards her. As the rescue ship came into sensor range, Marianne and her crew were underway to rendezvous with the rest of their flight to share the intelligence they had gathered and return home as rapidly as they could.

The good news was that the Vergazan assault fleet was still in the early stage of development. It was still on the ground and it was unlikely it would be into space, fully fitted and ready to make the long journey across the void for a decade or more. Periodic espionage missions from the earth solar system would check the progress of the Vergazan fleet.

Clear of any planets or residue from the local solar systems,

Marianne ordered Overlight Drive/maximum engaged returning them quickly to home base. From there Marianne made her way to SolSys Command HQ. At Command she presented the news of the Vergazan ships and of the potential allies that she had encountered.

The information was carefully considered. For the former, regular espionage missions would keep them abreast of the Vergazan fleet's progress. The latter presented a more difficult problem. Earth's pre-Lucie history pointed towards both the positive and negative aspects at arming potential allies. Still, these aliens with their limited technology and firepower were in a life and death struggle with a merciless foe in the Vergazan.

SolSys could certainly provide more sophisticated weaponry and technology without disclosing any significant advancements that had been made since the Vergazan threat had been discovered. The final decision of SolSys command and the planetary and communal councils was to provide some immediate weaponry and at the same time, offer the technological information to build more useful weapons and to vastly increase the speed and mobility of The Peoples', as the aliens called themselves, ships.

Those having more of the Lucie in their heritage retained some of the original Lucie abilities, most of which were partially lost with the development of the genotyping. A person who was predominantly of Lucie ancestry might be able to levitate across a narrow stream and stay dry as long as there were enough rocks above water to land on briefly. A person with more Lucie blood could survive under water perhaps long enough to swim from one end of an Olympic size pool to the other. The mixture of human and human/Lucie combined the scientific and technological mind of the Lucie along with diligence and perseverance with the human characteristics of canniness, social intelligence and reflexes. It was kind of like a street-smart kid from the hood who happens to have a graduate degree in Engineering.

The ones with this mixture made the best pilots, the best security officers, the sharpest military minds. They took the knowledge and understanding of the Lucie and merged it with the human tendency towards aggression. While war was never a consideration for the Lucies, the impending invasion of the Vergazan made it a necessity. The earthly human element had existed with the concept of war throughout its history creating among the mixed blood, warriors who would defend their home to the death. With the threat of war eliminated, these warriors, because of their Lucie blood, could then merge comfortably and quietly back into the civilization that they had built.

8

Dalkori, Titus and The Peoples' War Machines

Dalkori and Titus had been friends since childhood. Their earth human and Lucie ancestry were strong in them. On their native Europa under the cool distant sun and the warmth and light giving wormholes, they had built their forts and fought their battles against imaginary foe on the yet unsettled and undeveloped lands beyond the cities.

With the giant gas planet Jupiter looming above them, they dreamed of taking their Interstellar fighters deep into the hidden mists of Jupiter and rousting out the fantasy alien enemy hiding there ready to attack their home world. It was no surprise to anyone who had ever encountered them that they would join SolSys security, which they did. There they became excellent pilots and were top of their class in battle tactics. As cadets and Junior Officers there were few places in the solar system they had not participated in simulated combat under varying conditions.

Proud of their successes and almost hero status among their fellow officers, they were surprised to be called to the distant outpost of Charon. "Such a waste," many had said publicly, "for two such competent tacticians to be sent to patrol the frozen emptiness beyond the last planet and it's moon."

Stranger still, they were each appointed command of a cargo vessel that to their minds were little more than garbage scows. For two young men so highly proficient in combat tactics in one and two man interplanetary pursuit and space superiority fighters to be made commanders of clunky old cargo ships was seen as a serious demotion. Hour upon hour in a Charon Retail Community public house, they sat together over a cold beer and tried to figure out just what they had done wrong to have earned such punishment.

Never ones to flinch from duty, they guided their vessels through the outer colonies learning about their crews, learning to carefully and quickly load and unload whatever these colonies, many still in the early stages of terraforming, needed. For two long sidereal years they carried on this tedious and routine pursuit.

Had they really thought about it, they would have discovered that their piloting skill made them excellent at their jobs. Using their talent and the skill gained in the fighters, they were able to swing the huge, lumbering cargo vessels through amazingly tight quarters to dock, drop off and pick up all manner of cargo.

They were able to handle the long passages between the various outer colonies and grow comfortable with a crew that saw themselves as misfits and like Dalkori and Titus felt themselves to be unjustly slighted having been placed into positions they would never have chosen for themselves. The crew members like their commanders had been superior at their various jobs before themselves being sent to man those two old Charon based cargo vessels.

Given the routines, dull and tedious as they were, they were a little surprised as they unloaded a shipment of steel on one of Neptune's lesser moons to be ordered to fly deadhead directly to Pluto's SolSys base. Pluto's SolSys base was usually set aside as a place where senior officers on the way up could gain experience from Pluto control's high ranking veterans on their way out. They were ordered to the farthest two docks well away from the fancy yachts and state of the art vessels closer to the planet.

It had been considerable time since Dalkori and Titus had worn anything resembling a dress uniform. In their work fatigues, they couldn't have felt more out of place among senior command in their polished brass and their braided cuffs and collars and their admiralty brocade. A snappily attired young woman with the comet badges of a flight leader rushed up to them. She accepted salutes with a casual touch of her hand to her forehead. In a voice that didn't pull rank, she said, "Greetings gentlemen you are expected in the Admiralty Boardroom in five minutes. Follow me. I'll take you there."

Disconcerted and very curious they followed the flight leader down a long hall, no longer noticing the disparity in their dress from those around them.

The Admiralty Boardroom was ostentatious beyond any-thing they had seen since graduating from the academy back on Mars. The fact that it was on Pluto made it even more spectacular. The padded walls were covered with a silky gold material, the chairs surrounding the large real Earth Oak table appeared to be upholstered with leather. The Oak table was amazing. Real wood was a luxury well beyond the ability of most to acquire. Natural wood was limited to earth and a few plantations that had been established on Mars and two of the larger asteroids, Mapleoak and Woodlot. It must have cost a fortune to carry it here.

More awesome than any table, however were those entering through a door at the far end of the room. These were not up and comers, nor on the way outers. Wasn't that Admiral Marianne Mahone, risen in rank rapidly on her return from her mission across the void and her unexpected alien encounter. Two other Brigade Admirals joined her along with a number of lower ranks and three civilians.

All Dalkori and Titus could do was to stand firmly at attention holding a crisp salutes. "Gentlemen," said Admiral Mahone, "Please take a seat. As someone I have great respect for once said, 'this is not a bleepin' parade square.'"

"No doubt," said one of the Brigade Admirals, "you and your crews haven't been too happy with your current assignments. However, we must compliment you, for despite your displeasure, you have carried out your duties with efficiency and precision. We were sure you would, but we had to be certain."

The second Brigade Admiral took over, "We have been watching the two of you and your crews. We have seen your discouragement with your assignments first hand. We have also seen you, despite that, doing an excellent job. You have streamlined the delivery process and demonstrated superior skill in working with your crew and piloting those old and unwieldy vessels. You have given us exactly what we were looking for and more.

As of this moment, your ranks have both been raised to Flight Leader. Dalkori, you have been assigned the role of flight commander. No slight to you, Titus, the decision was random as either one of you have the competency, flight skill and leadership ability to assume the position. It is a requirement of

SolSys Security that each flight have a named commander. For all intents and purposes, you will share command anyway."

Dalkori turned to look a Titus, neither had a clue what the Admirals were talking about. The promotions, well beyond their current rank, were welcome although they had no idea why this honor was being bestowed on them. As to flight commander, they had no clue what that was about. They captained slow speed archaic freight carriers. The title and ranks were combat and security positions. Cargo vessels required no flight leaders or command titles.

Admiral Mahone looked at Dalkori and Titus and began to laugh, "Of course you have no idea what this is all about, do you?"

Dalkori and Titus looked at Admiral Mahone and simultaneously shook their heads. They were completely confused. The Admirals seemed to be talking about them, but it must be a mistake because Admiral Mahone was right, they had no idea what this was all about.

"The fact is," continued Admiral Mahone, "this meeting is all about you. You two have been assigned to the next journey across the void. With those of your crew that you consider capable and reliable, you will be piloting two state of the art Overlight plus cargo ships loaded with weapons and technology to rendezvous with The Peoples'.

You will be responsible for providing them with the advanced weaponry and technology. You will advise them regarding arming and increasing the potential speed of their existing ships. You will remain with The Peoples' until they have constructed several prototypes of the four person superiority fighters based on the technology we will have given them. Once they are combat ready, you will train them in planetary and interspace superiority tactics.

If you encounter a Vergazan ship you are permitted, with 'The Peoples' command approval, to engage. Once you are confident that The Peoples' fighter combat unit is ready, you may return home following a route similar that of the outward path to avoid detection of our presence by the Vergazan. If you encounter any Vergazan craft you must immediately engage and destroy. They must never suspect that we have achieved interstellar flight. Does this meet with your approval, or have you any questions?"

It did meet with their approval and the only question they had was enunciated by Dalkori, "When do we start?"

They were given two days to approve crew and since there were no slackers among them they had to resort to seniority and need to choose. The remaining were immediately cycled back to take on prime positions within their area of expertise each with a satisfying promotion and pay raise.

When they were first introduced to their ships the concept of cargo vessel took on a whole new meaning. These weren't the clunky rust buckets they had plied the outer planets supply routes with, but beautiful large streamlined vessels, fully equipped with the latest technology. That included the most current laser and projectile cannons. The interiors were well appointed with recreation space, gym, briefing room, and comfortable cabins for the crew. Each primary command bridge was elegantly designed for comfort and maximum efficiency. The backup bridge, deep in the bowels of each ship, intended for use only in the case of severe emergency, was more business-like.

Having taken the time to study and learn the layout of their ships, it was time to for Dalkori and Titus and their crews to move quarters from their old freighters onto their new ships. Once settled in they would begin putting the ships through their paces. First, however each commander and his crew were expected to give their ship a name. This was a tradition that had begun in the early days of terraforming. The spotters and shifters believing themselves to be working stiffs had decided their ships' identifying numbers, letters and symbols were too complicated to say or remember. Instead they chose to give their individual ships simple names.

Originally it was an attempt by these pilots to personalize their small space vehicles on which they would spend a considerable portion of their working lives. As terraforming spread, the number of spotters and shifters and other working vehicle increased to the point where it became necessary to keep track of them. The individual names provided for quick recognition and so SolSys began registering the ships by name.

Each new space vehicle was required to register a name within thirty earth days of activation. The pilot on the smaller vessels, or the pilot and crew of the larger ones would determine a name for their particular space craft, register it and write it on the hull in Lucie Prime, the written language of the pre arrival aliens and in English. Many added the name in one or more of the many earth languages particular to their culture of origin.

Since Dalkori and Titus were members of the extended Mahone family and since they would be following in the footsteps of the first two to cross the void to the distant arm of the galaxy, they decided, with the whole hearted approval of the crews to name their ships the Paddy and the Marianne. The Paddy was commanded by Titus and the Marianne by Dalkori. Printed on both sides of the ships, the names could be seen from many hundred kilometers away.

Dalkori and Titus tested their ships on the routes they had taken through the outer colonies where they had made deliveries with the interplanetary cargo vessels. What had taken them days in those ships, the Paddy and the Marianne, could do in a couple of hours at minimum Overlight speeds. Having become familiar with the handling of the ships at under and at minimum Overlight speeds, they then moved into empty space beyond Charon, out past most of the stray rocks at the outer planetary edge. There they practiced maneuvering at maximum Overlight speeds and made short warp jumps always with a focus on being combat ready no matter the situation.

Once everyone felt comfortable and confident under every flight condition, they made their way to Titan where the specialized supplies for The Peoples' was waiting to be picked up. Before long The Paddy and The Marianne were loaded with a large variety of armaments as well as dozens of near light drive engines and boxes of plans for building small quick and highly maneuverable four place Planetary Superiority ships.

Back on Charon, they were given the route they would take to meet up with The Peoples' while widely avoiding the Vergazan area of potential influence. The coordinates introduced to The Paddy and The Marianne's shipboard computers, they were ready for their first jump. A series of five jumps would bring them to the edge of stellar space where they would rendezvous with The Peoples'. Despite the fact that their route would take them far from the direct space lanes to their rendezvous to avoid the possibility of being detected by the Vergazan, the journey would still only take several weeks.

Engaging Overlight as they reached the first jump coordinates, the maximum drives kicked in and within moments they were travelling through the grey vagueness of warped space.

After several days of reviewing schematics and practicing jury rigging laser cannons and light drive engines, the crew was called to man battle stations. In a very short time, the ships were totally battle ready and stepped out of Overlight jump drive into normal space. It was dark and empty there and a quick scan of the area showed that there was nothing for millions of kilometers around them.

The ready horn sounded. With the second set of coordinates entered, the Overlight jump engines engaged and they were back in warping space. The crews returned to their duties. This was repeated three more times. The fifth and last jump ended with the crew at battle stations, but this time, they manned their positions with just a slight, extra edge to their preparedness. This time, the Paddy and the Marianne found themselves just off several sets of star systems. The stars were small and faint with one or two tiny rock planets and another set of gas planets. Further co-ordinates brought them to the nearest gas planet and put them into an orbit around one of the small moons closer to the planets cloudy outer surface than the others. There they waited as the time passed. Standard earth days became standard earth weeks until a standard earth month had passed.

Despite their training Titus, Dalkori and the crews of the Paddy and the Marianne were beginning to feel antsy. They wondered if they had somehow gotten the wrong coordinates for the rendezvous point. Was it possible that the Vergazan had broken The Peoples' scant defense forces, or that The Peoples' decided that they did not want assistance from the population of a far off solar system on another spiral edge of this vast galaxy?

Just as discouraged speculation was reaching its highest point among the crews of the Paddy and the Marianne, several vessels bearing the clumsy and slow pattern of The Peoples' defense force ships appeared on the extreme distance sensors. The crews of the Paddy and the Marianne watched impatiently as The Peoples' ships made, what seemed to them a plodding and stately progress toward the rendezvous site. It took them some time to recognize that The Peoples' ships were moving flat out at maximum speed. Their pace made it clear to Dalkori and Titus and to their crews that The Peoples' vessels, as they now were, would be sitting ducks for any hostile ship even if it only had a simple near light speed propulsion.

It was clear to Titus and Dalkori that even the dated technology they were carrying would vastly improve The Peoples' defense forces bringing them centuries forward and giving them a true fighting chance against the Vergazan who had stolen their worlds. The Vergazan who were in the process of systematically destroying them to develop an invasion force that could jump the gap between spiral arms of the galaxy and bring their destructive ways to the home communities of mother earth.

The Commanders and crews of The Paddy and The Marianne, watching the slow parade of their distant ally towards the rendezvous location, came to understand how absolutely crucial their mission was. They were not only offering hope to an alien species, but providing critical support for their own.

Each of the two large cargo vessels held a four man planetary superiority fighter similar to the structural design templates that they would be passing over to The Peoples'. Dalkori and three of his crew took the one from The Marianne and met up with The Peoples' small fleet as it set down on the rendezvous world.

The air, although thin and of slightly different composition was breathable and warm enough to permit a face to face meeting. The translation device worked even better than expected as The Peoples' figures of speech were not that different. The conversation didn't really take off until the Several Karidanz, including Master Debron and Over Cozi who commanded The Peoples' ships had a good look around and through the Planetary Superiority Fighter that would soon join their fleet. It was, however, the younger officers who were clearly enthused by the potential of such a machine.

Dalkori signaled for the two cargo ships to come down to the rendezvous and prepare for transfer of materials, weapons and engines. The transfer was relatively easy even for the heavier objects such as the Overlight one engines and the laser cannons as gravity on the chosen rendezvous site was about 0.3 of standard earth gravity and similar in relation to the home worlds of The Peoples'.

Admiral Mahone and the shipborne technology of her vessel had done a good job of describing the structure of the interior of the damaged ship she had encountered. Using these as starting points, the Technicians from the SolSys cargo ships were able to easily jury rig The Peoples' ships and install the engines they had brought with them. The Peoples' technicians while uncertain at first soon figured it out and worked alongside the humans installing cannons and engines.

The next job would be to train The Peoples' pilots how to control their now better armed, but more skittish ships. It took some time for many of them to become comfortable at the controls. The Peoples' vessels might look and basically, be the same ships, but, in fact, they were far different from the space craft they had come with. Most of the pilots struggled to keep their machines in line. It required delicate maneuvering to keep the ships from rapidly going from stop to Overlight speed, or take a sudden turn, or worse, an unexpected inversion. While most, even at slow speeds could barely control the ships. There were a few who seemed to take to it naturally.

Those few pilots and a few crew members that showed some natural ability with their vehicles joined Dalkori and Titus aboard the fighters. The Peoples' marveled at the speed and agility of these craft and the formidable firepower of the weaponry. A small number stayed behind when The Peoples' squadron of ships returned to their home bases with the plans and schematics for building more of their own weapons and constructing their four man fighters.

Those who remained where rigorously drilled in the fine art of flight and combat specific to these fighters. They first learned to control the flight characteristics adjusting yaw and roll and pitch, coming about quickly. They learned to fly comfortably within the gravity free environments of the ship. They discovered that they could achieve any possible attitude virtually instantaneously. Next they learned to control the shielding, a transparent cloak that deflected enemy weaponry, both ballistic and laser.

They were shown how to widen, tilt and manipulate the size and location of the shields. They practiced closing and opening firing ports and protecting themselves from incoming fire. After this they learned to coordinate their flight controls with their shields while in assault mode. They learned that should they fire a laser cannon when the shield was in front of it, it caused a blinding flash of light that could disorient them long enough for a hostile ship to make a serious or even potentially killing shot.

Strategy and tactics were practiced by having one ship, fully shielded. to prevent accidently damaging the ship or injuring the crew play the part of a Vergazan raider while the other tried to deliver a killing shot. The maneuverability of the ships allowed them to move from a flight or defensive condition to attack very quickly. Tactical training was relatively limited as the full capabilities of the Vergazan fighters were not known. Only direct contact with hostile fighters could teach The Peoples' fighter crews the most effective strategies to use against them.

By the time the first of The Peoples' fighter crews were fully trained and ready, new fighters were rolling off the assembly lines back on the few places that were The Peoples' remaining hideaways. A few of the early prototypes had been destroyed or damaged, more because of the limitations of the test pilots than because of the crafts themselves. The Peoples' crews trained by Dalkori and Titus and their flight teams returned to their hideaways where they would take on the roles of test pilots and trainers.

Given the distances between the stars and the arms of the galaxy and the time it required to develop the technology and build the vehicles that would allow one to travel freely between them, several earth standard years had passed before the cargo vessels were ready to return home. Dalkori and some crew members had volunteered to stay on to work in support of The Peoples' and the challenges they would face in their war effort. Titus and the remaining crews took the two cargo vessels home.

Following the return route set into their Overlight Jump Drives, The Paddy and The Marianne were back on Charon within two earth standard months. Titus was called to Pluto to meet with the SolSys Admiralty to debrief. He told of the success of retrofitting, training and creation of the fighters. He passed on the information that The Peoples' wished to send an ambassador toSol1's system as a liaison. This would have to be decided in the Great Legislature, but eventually ambassadorial ties would be extended to The Peoples'.

In the meantime, it was suggested that Titus return to the rendezvous site to inform The Peoples' that the decision regarding exchange of ambassadors was made and to evaluate the success of the previous mission and to offer some more updated technology to help in their fight. It took several years to prepare for this but eventually everything was worked out. Admiral Mahone, having been appointed first ambassador to The Peoples' Planetary Union and her family would accompany Titus on the journey.

The historic rendezvous site, was a small moon with breathable air orbiting a gas planet far closer to the sun than any gas planets in the Sol One system. The site had been chosen because of its nearness to the gas planet making it almost invisible, Titus and his passengers met up with key members of The Peoples' Diplomatic Corps.

The Peoples' had decided that the assistance they had received from the Sol One System government merited full honors for these important allies. Titus was guided to The Peoples' primary hideaway world that they called simply Exile One. As Titus ship came to rest just above the hard surface of the tarmac field, the dignitaries on board were able to take a moment to marvel at the hundreds of four-place Planetary Superiority Fighters, waiting for crew to be trained and take them up to meet the Vergazan, that were parked around them.

Not too far off where stone hills rose above the glass and steel buildings that suggested the heart of the military base,

Titus could see the fighters being put through their preflight inspections. Further along, some were already rising into the air. As the Ambassador to The Peoples', Marianne Mahone, her fellows of the SolSys diplomatic team and her family were lowered to the Tarmac, a flight of ten four-place fighters roared overhead half breaking to the left and half to the right as they passed over the ambassador. Ambassador Marianne Mahone returned the gesture with a stiff salute followed by a friendly wave.

At the initial briefing, Ambassador Mahone was pleased to hear that the four-place Superiority fighters had surprised a number of Vergazan combat ships and for the first time had been successful in defeating them. When the Vergazan seemed to initiate a major alert sending all their combat style craft to carry on a defensive posturing, traveling in large squadrons, The Peoples' decided to try a different tactic.

It was one that was proving very successful for The Peoples' and for them, much more rewarding than ship on ship battle. They had decided to carry the war to the very heart of the Vergazan war machine, the huge earth stripping plants that gathered the metals, the oils and the other valuable substances required for construction and propulsion of their growing fleet of invasion ships destined for Sol One System and beyond. Striking randomly, The Peoples' growing fleet of fighters and larger battle cruisers, now about to be vastly improved by the new technology brought in the form of blueprints and schematics aboard Titus' ship, had done sufficient damage by causing the Vergazan ship building to fall in to disarray. Due to The Peoples' battle tactics, the necessary materials the Vergazan used to build their great ships was growing scarcer.

For those back on the human worlds of Sol One System this

would be good news. It would mean a setback of Vergazan invasion plans for a good many years. But. no one human, Lucie or Peoples' could ever doubt that the Vergazan would ultimately persist in their plans to cross from one spiral arm of the galaxy to another with the intent of bringing their resource destroying machines to the Sol One System. Still, more time meant better defenses and there was some slight hope that The Peoples' might yet be able to salvage some of their planetary resources.

Even with the numbers of fighters and the growing assembly of battle cruisers, The Peoples' would never be able to penetrate the Vergazan defenses around the ship construction sites on what were formerly The Peoples' prime home planets. The ships would eventually be completed and the Vergazan would happily leave this sector of the universe and the pesky multitudes of The Peoples' fighters.

Although Vergazan command was amazed at the sudden technological advances of The Peoples', they were too arrogant to ever consider that they might have received help, especially from what they believed to be the primitive worlds of their next target, earth and her companion planets.

The Vergazan accepted what they determined was the ruth-lessness of The Peoples', for they, the ultimate bringers of planetary destruction, themselves, only knew brutality and ruthlessness. Because of their unbounded arrogance, brutality and ruthlessness, the Vergazan might have tried to invade the Sol One System even knowing what they were going up against. On the planets and communities of Sol One the plan was clear, the Vergazan Invasion could never be allowed to happen.

9

Deflectors

As best they could, The Peoples' kept up continuous attacks on the Vergazan extra planetary resource gathering. Their prime targets were the strip and deep earth mining automatons, crystalline and nuclear materials gathering processors that recklessly tore through hundreds of thousands of square kilometers of potentially productive land. With a ruthless disregard of what the land might have been, whether home to valuable forest, farms and villages, towns and cities. the Vergazan mining processors took everything of value to well below bedrock. While doing this, the machines leached all the nutrients from the soil leaving a barren land where countess centuries might pass before anything would ever grow again.

The Peoples' forces targeted those massive machines with a vengeance. It was their homes these machines destroyed. Huge laser cannons on The Peoples' earth designed battle cruisers pounded the mining processors wherever they could. Four place and more recent two place fighters fought off the Vergazan airborne defenses while adding their own formidable fire power against the processors.

These attacks closed down a large number of the mining and resource gathering operations, forcing the Vergazan to limit them to places where they could sustain a strong defense posture. While The Peoples' were saving numerous planets moons and larger asteroids from destruction, they were outnumbered and out gunned when it came to rescuing their home planets. The best The Peoples' could do was to mount random small scale attacks, getting in, inflicting the most damage they could under the circumstances, then getting out before too many Vergazan defenders arrived.

Besides harassing the Vergazan ship construction they were able to gather ongoing and useful intelligence about the progress of the invasion fleet. A number of the massive invasion ships were now being lifted into orbit for final fittings and testing. The Peoples' forces had been able to damage several and destroy one or two, while passing on the word through the SolSys diplomatic team back to Sol One security command that the Invasion ships were being readied.

SolSys had used the time The Peoples' offensive had bought them well. They had developed a whole array of defensive weaponry that they hoped would clear the threat of the Vergazan from this entire sector of space. Wormhole technology had advanced to where they could be used as portals sending whole ships to the far reaches of the universe and possibly to totally new sets of universes. The latter was only speculation as no one had cared to investigate. In nearly every case the wormhole would close and reopen on a new location allowing no opportunity for a return trip.

Besides the various useful, functional and defensive wormholes, the most exciting development of modern wormhole technology was the 'deflector' The deflector distorted space itself. A space ship encountering a deflector would be instantly warped back several light years to where they had been prior to encountering it. There were no limits to the number of times a deflector could send a ship back to where it came from.

Since a deflector was in essence a spatial field, its only limit was determined by the generator and the field buoys that marked its two dimensional spatial limits. Research and development of the deflector came quickly on the heels of the first prototype. By the time the Vergazan were in the final stages of launching their armada for theSol1 System, a deflector field rectangular in shape covered as much as thirty light years of area at the edge of the arm of the galaxy from whence the Vergazan would set out. This was the route they would have to take to reach earth's solar system in the least amount of time and with the least expenditure of fuel.

The scientists and military tacticians back in the Sol1 Sys were well aware that eventually the Vergazans would find a way around the deflector. That was something that would take more time and the Vergazan's new routes and need to spread their fleet out would eliminate some aspects of the principles of surprise the Vergazan preferred. They would have to take position just beyond the last planets of the system and regroup before beginning their assault

The Vergazan were too powerful to be stopped by what they considered to be a less developed civilization. This thinking was based on the fact that the Vergazan had yet to encounter an enemy as capable as themselves, scientifically, tactically, or in singularity of purpose. The only thing that would be of even a slight concern to them was the expenditure of fuel that a change in tactics such as a spread out and circuitous pathway to their planned target might entail.

Reports were coming toSol1 that the Vergazan fleet was in its entirety in space and receiving final fittings. The fleet would soon be on its way. The Peoples' were able to harass the fleet forcing the Vergazan to launch large numbers of small fighters to keep The Peoples' ships at bay. The efforts of the Vergazan fighters to protect their mother ships proved to be at a great cost and by the time the fleet was ready to depart that part of the galaxy hundreds of Vergazan fighters and their crews had been lost.

Ultimately and as expected, the Vergazan did succeed in driving back the bulk of The Peoples' assault ships. As the Vergazan fleet moved free of the influence of those solar systems on which they had encroached and ruined over many earth centuries, The Peoples' watched and waited for their moment to reclaim their home worlds.

The small group of humans who spent time among The Peoples' as the ambassadorial team celebrated along with The Peoples' in their joy. They also watched the Vergazan fleet as it began its journey beyond the star systems of that arm of the galaxy. And, they knew it's intention.

10

The Invasion Launch Begins Again and Again

The humans of the ambassadorial team to The Peoples' knew where the Vergazan fleet was headed and its intentions in doing so. They immediately sent a warning to the home defense of Sol1Sys informing them of the Vergazan's progress. The moment the Vergazan fleet engaged their version of overlight drive, the deflector was ready. With the deflector's encounter with the Vergazan armada scant days away, the SolSysOne observers stood by to report the success or failure of earth's massive initial defense.

They watched twenty-seven massive war ships flanking a much larger Queen ship that was the control center, the "brains" of the operation. Each ship had an escort of seven battle cruisers. As they began engaging their version of overlight drive, the ships appeared to elongate, then a tiny pinpoint of light appeared at the leading edge of each vessel seeming to instantly suck them into darkness and then, the pinpoint and the ships were gone.

Within minutes of surpassing light speed, they would encounter the deflector. If everything worked as expected, most of the ships would wind up right back where they started, and drop into sub-light propulsion. As many times as they tried to proceed to greater than light speed, they would vanish only to return to somewhere near their starting point. For the lead ships, there would be a moment when they would find themselves at the rear of their own armada at the moment those enormous vessels entered into above light speed. The deflected ships would see those ships for just a split second. Seconds later, the lead ships would resume faster than light speeds only to be sent back again.

To the delight of the human and The Peoples' viewing the departure, the lead ships began to rapidly reappear near where they had been when they engaged their version of overlight drive. Some of the lead ship commanders unexpectedly discovering ships ahead of them reacted by firing on them. The fired-on ships, not expecting anyone behind them returned fire. There was a brief chaotic battle in which several of the massive Vergazan ships were destroyed or immobilized by their own.

While the Vergazan did not understand how this was happening, they eventually figured out they were being cycled back to their starting points. The Armada now reduced to twenty-four functional ships after many deflections were ordered by the Queen ship to stop and regroup. Believing themselves to be victimized by some mysterious space anomaly, never suspecting it might be purposeful or considering that those they were intending to invade were advanced to this level, battle cruisers were withdrawn from escort and deployed to find some way around it.

Finding the way around the deflector was not an easy task. On a regular basis, battle cruisers were being flung back among the larger ships. Some of both the larger and smaller craft where damaged and some battle cruisers even destroyed in collisions with other battle cruisers and the huge assault ships. After some time, the command came from the Queen ship for the gigantic assault ships to draw back and shut down all but emergency power to prevent any further dissipation of critical fuel.

They set up coordinated orbits around any space object they could find including each other to prevent drifting apart or the possibility of a degenerate orbit that might see an inopportune fall into atmosphere. Any of these massive ships landing on a planet, especially one with an atmosphere, would require a huge expenditure of energy to return to viable space. The Vergazan pilots were skilled enough to maintain successful orbits and only one ship was forced to burn off fuel to clear atmosphere.

Meanwhile, the battle cruisers were continuing to bounce back in large numbers. Slowly they began to approach the solution to their dilemma. One of the battle cruisers that came too close to one of the buoys supporting the deflector had to be destroyed before it could communicate back to the waiting fleet.

The Vergazan were not sentimental. Their only concern despite the disappearance of a battle cruiser, as with the damaged and destroyed ships within the flotilla, was with diminishment of attack capability. They quickly and ruthlessly salvaged what they could from any badly damaged ship. No one really cared about their countless and ultimately replaceable fellows slowly freezing to death or suffocating as heat and atmosphere from their compromised vessels bled off into the frigid wastes of space.

More than five sidereal earth years would pass before the Vergazan were able to map out some ways around the deflector, certain that they had found the limits of the space anomaly that held up their invasion plans. They were now prepared to proceed.

There were no direct routes that would take them past the space distortion of the deflector, and bring them directly to theSol1 solar System. The ships would have to travel many light years out of their way before turning towards their target. They would also have to regroup before entering the system.

A singular mass invasion was a tactic the Vergazan used should the system they were invading have some way to observe their arrival. Such a ploy was guaranteed to terrify, confuse and otherwise upset the populations of the inhabited worlds long before the ships arrived over their heads. According to the knowledge they had been fed, this was such a solar system, primitive and ill-prepared for the superiority of the Vergazan conquerors.

The humans onSol1 System, earth and its many surrounding communities were confident that the Vergazan threat was more than well under control. There was concern for some of the slowly developing communities among the most recently terraformed gas planet moons and those being terraformed that had been blasted up from the rocky cores of Neptune and Saturn.

The more developed of the space communities among the gas planet moons could muster their own defense with the support of the SolSys security forces and be absolutely protected from stray attacks by the Vergazan invaders. The newer ones were more likely to be susceptible to the firepower that even the small Vergazan fighters could bring to bear.

SolSys interplanetary superiority fighter groups and several detachments of Marines were stationed on some of these newer communities, ones that had some population. Various sizes of gunships provided routine oversite for those newly terraformed or in the process of being terraformed and as of yet, unpopulated or limited to members of terraforming crews.

Most of the Vergazan fleet were making their way around the deflector. While some still found themselves back at their starting point only to lose more time recalibrating before finally clearing the deflector. SolSys Security was fully aware of where all the invader's vessels were, of how many there were, how many, including battle cruisers, had been lost. They counted six of the massive mother ships and ninety-two battle cruisers were lost to the Vergazan fleet. This left a still massive invasion force of twenty one mother ships and the Queen ship.

At the moment the invasion force looked pretty ragtag, Security knew that when the time came they would be facing the full brunt of the invaders. Deflectors, redirectors, and wormhole carriers were ready for that moment. The command of theSol1 System knew that these would eliminate the bulk of the Vergazan ships and forces, but they also understood that they were facing a ruthless enemy. To the last, the Vergazan would be relentless in wreaking as much destruction as they could right down to a personal level. SolSys fighters and ground based defenses were armed to the teeth with a whole variety of weaponry, from ballistic, to laser, and the relatively new disrupters that could fragment an enemy at the molecular level and were adjustable for either long distance defense or for fighting at close quarters.

Most hoped that it would never come to that. The combined Lucie, human heritage was by nature non-violent, but would not hesitate to protect family, friends, and fellow humans if need be. They were all well-aware that no matter how much they might have wished for a better way, they could give the invaders no quarter.

When the Vergazan mother ships formed their series of heptagons hiding the Queen ship in their midst along with the incomplete heptagon of the two extra ships, five already lost and destroyed lined up in the fourth position to begin their assault, the SolSys wormhole carriers were ready.

These were large ships in their own right but remained totally concealed by the portals they carried. To the observers aboard the Vergazan, all that they could see was the empty space within the Wormholes' huge maws. Even as they broke through into the influence of the solar system, they would have no idea of the presence of the ships and their enormous space tunnel openings.

The Vergazan sensed no threat as they increased power creating what they thought to be a terrifying presence racing in towards the sun. So intent on their theatrical performance to spreading horror and the sense of inadequacy among the unprepared of earth eight of their number had encountered the wormhole carriers and had already been dispersed to some far off spot across the universe. Until then there was not the slightest suspicion among Vergazan command it might be them, not the earth, who were inadequate and unsuspecting. Still, they were arrogant enough to press their plunge into the heart of the solar system. Their only defensive behavior was to launch their vast squadrons of fighters and have the battle cruisers engage the still invisible enemy.

At this point, the human/fighter support joined the fray to protect the ships carrying the space tunnel generators.

Countless dogfights formed and dispersed as Solsystem's space superiority class fighters proved their superior speed and firepower.

While Vergazan battle cruisers fearlessly and ferociously attacked every human vessel they could find, they were on every level outclassed. From the bridge of the wormhole or space tunnel generators crew members watch as their prey, the huge mother ships tried to evade the gaping mouth of the wormhole only to be inexorably sucked in, slowly stretching towards the gaping wormhole mouth then begin to shrink as evasion proved pointless and they rapidly disappeared from view, their battle cruisers and fighters being drawn after them like so much flotsam and jetsam.

Still a great distance from the heart of the system, barely even among the furthest out communities. The mother ships of the Vergazan fleet vanished one by one into the distant regions of space, possibly even into new dimensions. Those that were able to survive the forces within the wormholes found themselves to be scattered and alone in distant and unfamiliar regions of space. Countless millennia would pass before any one of the Vergazan mother ship communities could ever be able to mount even a local invasion assuming they could find suitable worlds to ravish.

Back in SolSystem the only vessel still present, the Queen ship was now trying desperately to flee back into the void between the distant arms of the solar system, Besides launching their fleet of numerous fighters and using their cruiser escort to fight a rear action. They had also put out the call to any of their remaining combat vessels fighters and cruisers that had avoided the drop into the wormhole along with their mother ships to join the Queen to guard, protect and do battle on her behalf and to assist in any way possible to aid in her escape.

The influence of the wormholes carried by the SolSys ships was slightly less than a thousand kilometers wide and beyond that diameter its pull faded. The giant computers aboard the Queen ship had observed through their long range sensors some of the SolSys fighters using the influence of wormholes to radically change directions and slingshot off at very high speed. The information was immediately programmed into the computers of their own fighters and battle cruisers.

Using the new information squadrons of Vergazan fighters were dispatched to engage the Space tunnel projector ships. Using the pull of the wormhole to build speed, then at the moment before absorption they would maximize power, veering to left or right and spinning past the edge of the space tunnel and confront the carrier, cannons blazing. As simple as that sounded, it wasn't. The carriers' superior sensors immediately anticipated the arrival of the Vergazan fighters and would instantly begin firing their disrupters.

The Vergazan fighters, depending on where they arrived to face the carriers' broadsides had learned enough about the disrupters' destructive firepower with information from the dying fighters and some of those that had escaped with minimal damage. They had been able to gauge the range of the disrupter projectors and would set their slingshot course off the wormholes to bring them broadside, but out of range of the carrier's disrupters.

This presented two problems for the Vergazan fighters and the few battle cruisers that were sent to attack the wormhole carriers. The first problem was that the range made accurate laser fire nearly impossible dissipating in the defensive honeycomb sheeting of the SolSys ships while missing the few penetrable areas into the interior and the power centers. This meant that they could inflict minimal damage to the carriers.

It also meant that within moments the superiority fighters of the SolSys defenders were there to engage them. Fierce fighter to fighter combat would ensue, the Vergazan fighters, marginally slower and less maneuverable than the SolSys craft, were ultimately destroyed or driven off in tatters.

To be sure, the Vergazan fighters were never that easy to destroy or drive off. They were persistent and in many cases ruthless to the extreme and often in desperation resorted to kamikaze tactics. The real problem was the numbers of Vergazan fighters. Each Mothership and battle cruisers together could deploy tens of thousands of fighters. While most followed the larger ships into the wormholes, many didn't. Most of the battle cruisers and fighters that had lost their Motherships joined the Queen ship with its own forty-nine battle cruisers and multiple thousand fighters. Dog fights hardly described the interaction of SolSys combat vessels, destroyers and fighters with the Vergazan battle cruisers and the countless Vergazan fighters. A better term might be a prison yard melee.

11

The B0B-C Twins

Tighe

Tighe Saunds was born on Titan, one of the larger, and despite its great distance from earth, one of the earlier developed communities. The first of two gigantic solar wormholes provided enough heat and light to the surface to create a large semitropical zone and more moderate zones to each side that extended outwards to desert polar regions. A twenty-seven hour journey along an equatorial ground transportation route would carry the traveler around the moon and back to the starting point. Irregular land routes added another two days to circumnavigate its entire longitudinal axis.

Apart from the inner planetary communities, Titan was one of the larger man made communities. It had a well-established population by the time of the Vergazan invasion. Three large cities and numerous smaller towns could be found near the three large, interconnected lakes that spread around the surface relatively near the equator. Smaller lakes and streams that maintained the temperate zone surrounded a variety of agricultural communities. And while the desert areas due to their dryness and their cooler temperatures were not popular places to live, still tiny villages could be seen dotting the grasslands that bordered them. In one of these small villages, not far from a large temperate zone town, Tighe's family had made their home.

Tighe could claim a distant family relationship with the infamous Marianne Mahone, Admiral of the SolSys fleet and first ambassador to an alien species and her older brother, Paddy, the first to come across the potential invaders while working as a SolSys security officer in the asteroid belt. Just as Paddy had loved his freedom to explore the then unsettled areas of Mars around his home town, Tighe loved his freedom to explore the sparsely settled area around his home.

As a student, he had taken trips to the edge of the desert and even visited one of the larger cities where he and his class were able to take a wormhole journey to Mars. Although they never got beyond the grand viewing concourse that looked out on distant Barsoom City and the souvenir shops that lined it, they could claim to all their fellow schoolmates that they had been to Mars, "Yeah, it was OK. Barsoom City is pretty big, I guess."

It wasn't until Tighe was about 15 in earth years that he realized what he wanted to do with his life. He was laying in the grass near his home, looking up at the stars when a four vessel SolSys fighter training squadron broke through the atmosphere to do a low and over and came screaming across the sky so close to where Tighe was that he almost felt he could reach up and touch them. He jumped to his feet to follow them with his eyes before they swiftly disappeared beyond the horizon. At that moment, he decided that he wanted to be a fighter pilot and fly one of those incredible machines.

The next few years found Tighe amazing his family, friends and teachers alike with his new-found studiousness and academic diligence. Toward the end of his final term he submitted an application for SolSys Cadet school on Mars. It was a school based on a variety of military colleges from years back that was affectionately known as "The Point".

A historical movie buff might understand the reference, but few others, including the cadets had any idea of the origin of the name. Most retained their ignorance, except for those cadets who paid attention during the introductory presentation on the opening day of each freshman cadet class. In that first lecture, the new cadets would learn that their school got its name from a historically renowned institution that had existed in the earth nation called the United States.

Back on earth this institution was a military academy designed to send highly efficient and well trained officers into leadership roles. The graduates moved confidently into whatever field of warfare that interested them, actual combat, planning or politics. The training they received would help them excel whatever they took on. This military academy was distinguished by the excellent quality of its graduates as well as through countless references in books and movies.

The Point, was not on earth and not featured in countless books or movies. It had, however, been referenced in several current videos and works of fiction. Its goal was not necessarily to produce military, planning or political leaders as much as it was intended to militarize a group of citizens willing to fly tiny machines at breakneck speed through the solar system and if necessary through the vast reaches of space with, as the Vergazan Invasion loomed, the intention of wreaking total destruction of the solar system's soon to arrive enemies. This was something quite uncharacteristic of the new humanity of the Sol1 System.

Tighe, despite the fact that there wasn't a malicious bone in his body, had been enamored of the fighters he had seen over Titan. He fell absolutely in love with the tiny, lightning fast and highly maneuverable gunships the moment he climbed into one.

The Point was difficult, but Tighe worked hard. The intense labor of study was broken only by those moments in flight school. From the first rough journey aboard a simulator it was confirmed that Tighe's skill was flying. He was thrilled by his first flight on board a subspace trainer with its vertical takeoff and its high speed attitude changes. Far more sophisticated and functional than any vertical takeoff jet of the early twenty-first century, it still required significant skill to fully control the attitude and land on the variety of surfaces over which the training sessions were held.

The first flight beyond the atmosphere was very exciting for Tighe. He practiced as often as he could, launching from The Point air station and carrying low gravity maneuvers over the training and testing site on Phobos, Mars' smaller moon. By the time live ordinance was added to the extra planetary trainers, Tighe was an expert, easily making the various targets, both long range ones and those that seemed to suddenly appear near his craft.

Although this is where he wanted to be, Tighe was still obliged to spend intense hours at the technical and academic studies the SolSys command felt was crucial to the development of anyone who was to man any one of their different kinds of extra-terrestrial vehicle. To this end, Tighe found himself piloting everything from a freighter to ten and twenty crew battle cruisers. For four long years Tighe dreamed of the day when he would finally pilot a two crew space superiority fighter, an amazingly fast and deadly craft that was the pride of the SolSys space force.

While there was no guarantee that Tighe would be assigned to this sweet craft, he did everything he could to show that he belonged in the cramped cockpit of the tiny B zero class space superiority vessel, the fastest and most efficient fighting ship in the SolSys fleet.

Corinne

Corinne Brindar entered The Point the same year as Tighe. He saw her as being something rare and remote, almost alien in that she was from earth.

With the diaspora to the planets and distant space colonies, earth's population had stabilized at about four and a half billion. Most of the earth population were scientists and technocrats and the people who served them.

For most dwellers within the solar system, earth was little more than a walk away through a wormhole portal. However, being the origin for all the system communities, it was seen as nearly mythic. It was the home world, the place where humanity and Lucies first met and the dream of populating the entire system was born. The rest of the system's population believed that the citizens of earth were by and large wealthy and lived on huge estates that bordered enormous cities. This was an exaggeration, that was rooted in some truth.

The citizens of earth, being the scientists, technologists and planners along with those who served them did tend to be somewhat wealthier than most. There were very few estates. Most lived in townhouses in small communities and commuted to work.

Corinne's family included technicians and shop keepers as well . She had lived there with her parents, a younger brother. An older brother was already ahead of her at The Point training to be a fighter pilot at the time she entered.

The family home was in the north west of the North American continent where the nations of the United States and Canada were once found. To be sure, the citizens still referred to themselves as citizens of these historical nations although the social changes had long made separate nations obsolete. No place on the entire planet was more than five minutes away. Still, to the cadets at The Point, Corinne and the other earthlings, as they were called, were seen as being exotic and unapproachable.

Tighe remembers seeing Corinne at the opening ceremonies their first year. He thought that she was cute, but among those from the terraformed communities, particularly the outer worlds, the cadets from earth were believed to be different and they generally avoided them. The earth cadets tended to stick together. This was however, a fairly general phenomenon. The Martians tended to stick together as well and so did those for the Asteroid Belt communities, some of which were quite small. Those from the Outer Worlds tended to hang around together as well. The intermingling was confined to the class rooms and lecture halls.

Over the years in the academy Tighe had shared several classes with her. He knew from those classes that she was very smart, usually top of the class. What he didn't know was that she was as enamored of flying as he was. She, too, worked hard to achieve the right to fly one of the new BB intersystem superiority class fighters.

Like Tighe, this was what she dreamed of and she became a highly skilled pilot as well. Still, come graduation, she had no more idea of where she would end up than Tighe did. There were a variety of vessels that required skilled pilots and until the post-graduation marshaling none of the cadets would have any idea what kind of vessel they would be assigned to.

As graduation approached and the Vergazan fleet was preparing to launch their invasion, none of the cadets doubted that they would, at some point, encounter the enemy no matter what sort of ship they might find themselves flying. The Point's graduating cadets were military. They would handle the war machines while the mercantile service would man the transports and freighters. There was, however, no certainty as the military arm of SolSys had grown quite large and had a wide variety of space craft that needed pilots including transports and freighters.

Graduation day was exciting as the cadets received their star and comet badges indicating that they were full ensigns, but the real anticipation was towards the marshaling when they would be assigned their place on one of the many vessels of war. They might have been pacifists by nature, but all were eager to take their places in any one of a half dozen kind of killing machine.

Their star and comet badges still fresh upon their collars, they were no longer cadets, but full officers, Ensigns of the SolSys battle fleet. They were marched through the broad corridor of the Mars, Phobos space tunnel to the tiny Martian moon where the marshaling would take place. From there they would be distributed around the system to the locations where their particular ships awaited.

There were moments of high anxiety and moments filled with long sighs of relief as groups of the young officers were identified and given their assignments, loud enough for all to hear: "Inner space SolSys cruisers. Ensign Rondal Smitts, navigator, Ensign Tara Rafinigan, gunnery officer, Ensign Anita Smollet, pilot, " and so on.

Let's Do the Twist

For what seemed to Tighe to be an interminable amount of time, the assignment and roll call for each variety of combat type vessel droned on. They had reached the part of the marshaling when the groups manning the Space Tunnel Projectors were being called separately, based on the unit number of the ship they would be joining. There were still a significant number of un-placed officers when Tighe heard his name called. He had not been designated a status, or a ship but was ordered to join a group at a numbered wormhole. Corinne joined that group as she and Tighe made their way to the wormhole gate indicated.

With little more to do than stand there as a second and much larger group was being called forward, Tighe counted those who stood somewhat aimlessly around him. He wasn't exactly certain but he thought there might be around sixty others in his particular group. A couple of his acquaintances from The Point had joined him to talk in hushed and nervous tones about where they were destined to be assigned. "Garbage Patrol, no doubt," said one of the wags in a slightly louder than intended voice.

There was some nervous laughter, but most were too lost in their own anxiety to notice. The roll call for the second group finally came to an end. Across the central podium Tighe could see a crowd of what must have been about 200 of his fellow ensigns standing around a second Space tunnel gate.

The commander at the podium called them to order. "B zero B-AA, B zero B-AB, and B zero BB interspatial superiority fighter candidates will follow Squadron Leader Torgeson and Group Commander Smithee, raise your hands please, to base Calisto where you will be placed in operational pairings and assigned flight duties."

As the large group began to disappear into the wormhole passage. Those around Tighe, including Corinne looked dejectedly at their feet. The fighter element was on its way to Calisto. Perhaps this group was really bound for garbage duty. The commander at the podium did not give them any time for self-pity. "Ladies and gentlemen you will proceed through the space tunnel to Charon. There you will be assigned to operational pairing and receive your sub-lieutenant's pip as pre-active members of the elite B zero B-BC and B zero B-CC Interstellar superiority fighter groups."

"Not too shabby," said Tighe to no one in particular. "assigned to an elite squadron and getting a promotion all in the space of 24 earth hours."

"Not too shabby, for sure, " came the response in a female voice with a light earth accent.

Turning to see who had spoken, Tighe found himself looking at the smiling face of Corinne. "You're Tighe, I've heard that you are a pretty good pilot. I'm Corinne."

Tighe found that he was at a loss for words. That only lasted a moment, "Hi Corinne. I expect everyone with us are all pretty good pilots,"

He was really tongue tied this time, " I mean including you, of course."

She just laughed and continued marching. When they reached the assembly hall on Charon, several young men at tables were handing out sub-lieutenant's pips. As one of them handed the pips to Tighe and Corinne he said, "You're sub-lets now. You can put those on your dress uniforms, they look great, and then you can put them in your closet and go back and check them every once in a while. Doesn't look as fancy stamped on your combat fatigues which you'll be getting shortly as soon as you are paired to a 'twister'."

"Twister?" asked Corinne.

"I think command calls them Interstellar Superiority Fighters. Not sure, haven't heard that name in a long time."

The talkative one behind the table may have had more to say, but by then Tighe and Corinne were well beyond him and looking for familiar faces to join up with.

There was little time to do this as a screen at the front of the assembly hall lit up showing a diminutive female in combat fatigues standing behind a small dais. "Officers, may I have your attention please. I am Wing Leader Shyanne Garriger and I must say, you look resplendent in your sub-lieutenants' pips. You will have about three standard earth hours to enjoy them, after pairing and a welcoming dinner, you will be changing into combat fatigues like this." as she indicated her uniform, " and they will become your day to day wear while you are on this station. Your first official briefing will be directed by your flight commander, who will be your mother, father and annoying elder sibling for the next couple of months. You will be meeting with them in about four standard earth hours from now. Check the boards for your room and pairing assignment. Have a great dinner and get ready to get down to business."

The dinner was great. Tighe doubted that he had ever seen such a spread even back home during those famous Titan food fests. Those gigantic communal banquets that had become a tradition on Titan harking back to the days before terraforming was complete and permanent solar wormholes had been established. As Saturn moved between Titan and the sun, there was a period of time when the electrical systems supplying residences would be very limited especially during a full eclipse. The planetary axis Titan took around Saturn generally made this a fairly short time, but it was usually long enough to compromise foodstuff in refrigerators and freezers. In the early days just before Saturn and Titan crossed paths blocking the view of the sun. people would clear out their cold storage and share what they had with their neighbors.

Later when the solar wormholes were stabilized and more modern technology was able to sustain the power at optimal even during the eclipses, people continued to carry on the tradition of the communal sharing. Entrenched in the life of the citizens of Titan, it took on the status of a social festival and was reputed throughout the solar system as a major event and well worth making one's way to Titan to enjoy.

There was always a plethora of food, as neighborhoods vied with each other to set out the best spread to draw locals and tourists alike to their particular feast. This rivalry created a gourmet's paradise and for a period of approximately two and a half earth weeks, it was the place to be for any gourmand, or, for that matter, anyone who loved fabulous and often exotic food.

For Tighe who preferred flying to feasting usually stayed close to home to share with his family during the festival days. The food set out for the new recruits may well have been more than he had seen during the pre-eclipse festival on Titan. What was more, he felt at home among his peers, many of whom he knew from his time at The Point. The Mess Hall was a happy. noisy place that day. "Eat up and enjoy it," said the veterans of the base, "You won't be seeing anything like this until the next batch of newbies arrive next year."

The meal finished, the so-called newbies were back in the assembly hall to look up their room assignments and find out who they would be sharing the cockpit of their assigned 'twisters' as the veterans called the Superiority Fighters they would be flying.

As Tighe was searching through the list of rooms to find his names, he heard one of his buddies from The Point saying, "Well now, lookee whose next door to the freakin' steam zephyr from earth."

"I haven't got time for that stuff," said Tighe, still searching through the enormous list of room assignments, "There's an invasion coming and all I care about is being ready for that."

"Yeah, well take a glance at room assignments one and two," exclaimed Tighe's buddy.

Even in his rush to find his allotted place and get down to business, he looked up to discover his name beside room number two. The name beside room number one was Sub-Lieutenant Corinne Brindar. It looked as if he was the one living next door to the freakin' steam zephyr from earth.

"How the hell did that happen?" Tighe asked no-one in particular.

"Come on over to the assignment board," said Tighe's buddy, "I think I can show you the answer."

Tighe stood staring at the duty roster, his assignment list. He was speechless to see that he had been teamed with Corinne

Brindar. It took his buddy to further point out that he and Corinne has been named team leaders of the B0B-C squadron.

Tighe was overwhelmed. The last thing in the world he would ever have imagined was being named a team leader and that his co-pilot and fellow team leader was the very popular freakin' steam zephyr earth girl that he had so carefully avoided as an unnecessary distraction over the past four years at The Point.

While Tighe continued to gaze at the assignment roster, he began to think how he might go about changing his assignment or at least getting a new partner, hopefully one of his Titan-born friends. As he stood there lost in thought, he heard a voice from behind, "So you're the guy teamed with my sister."

Tighe turned to see a tall young first lieutenant looking at him, "Be good to her, she's not used to you out worlders. Hurt her and I'll see to it that it doesn't happen a second time."

"I'm not going to hurt anyone," said Tighe, "I'm going to ask for a transfer to another team. So, you don't have to worry, she won't be contaminated by an outworlder, at least not this one."

"You're going to get a transfer," grinned the first lieutenant, "I'd like to see that. The only kind of transfer you'd get is onto an ambulance, or cargo ship. Guess you haven't met SL Garriger our esteemed leader and ice lord. Nope, no transfers within group, just out. See you around 'subby' and remember what I said."

He turned away to join up with two other First Lieutenants who had been standing nearby and was gone. They were laughing rather loudly as they disappeared into the crowd. Tighe was left more confused than ever. He would ask for the transfer anyway, "Really now, ambulance or cargo tub."

Tighe was cocky enough to know he was a fighter pilot not

a space tub conductor. Looking around he saw a large portal that many of the people in the room were headed to. Above the archway, printed in Bold block letters were the words, fighter team accommodations and scramble rooms A, B, C.. Following the crowd, Tighe was able to find his room. He found his fatigues on his bed. He took off his dress tunic, dress shirt and tie and the pressed dress pants with the red and yellow stripe down the side of each leg and put them, along with his sub lieutenant's pips where they would stay for a very long time.

The combat fatigues although not quite form fitting were designed to be flexible enough for normal and even strenuous activity on the ground yet could be merged with a pilot's vacuum safe anti-freeze flight suit for flight missions. The extremely tough, but soft boots could slip easily inside a pair of specially matched boots creating a hermetic seal with the flight suit. Within minutes, someone like Tighe would be ready for a spacewalk feeling neither the pressure nor the absolute frigidity of the vacuum of space.

Tighe was just finished dressing when a soft voice began emitting from a tiny speaker on the wall near the door, "Newly arrived sub Lieutenants, group C," it said, "you are to proceed to lecture hall immediately. Follow the yellow lights on the floor. They will direct you to the lecture hall that is on your left through the Scramble Room."

Tighe opened his door to see Corinne, making her way along the corridor following the yellow directing lights. He closed his door and waited a moment before stepping out into the hallway giving Corinne enough time to get well ahead of him. The halls were crowded with a large group of his fellow new arrivals following the yellow lights while some others followed green lights and still others a set of mauve lights. The yellow lights guided Tighe to an open door beside which were the words, "brief, debrief and lecture, group c."

Inside the large theatre-like room new arrivals were milling around, checking out the numbers on the rows of seats. A senior officer on a podium with a microphone in his hand, kept repeating, "Please, take the seat that has your room number. They are numbered sequentially in rows of twenty."

Feeling quite uncomfortable, Tighe made his way to seat number two right beside Corinne. She turned and gave him a nice smile, but didn't get to speak to him as the briefing had begun. It was mostly about pride, selflessness and the training schedule was handed out to each before the flight commander in charge of their flight, FC Eddon Dentan, officially dismissed them and told them not to stay up too late because the fun was going to start very early the next morning.

Gathering his courage, Tighe ignored Corinne who was trying to speak to him and walked away from her towards FC Dentan. "Sir," he said coming to attention in front of his commanding officer and snapping a brisk salute, "I would like to speak with you."

"No problem Sub Lieutenant," he replied with a more casual salute, "Forget the sir stuff. call me Cappy, all the rest of them do. I keep forgetting to take my hat off in the senior officers' mess so I've ended up buying more rounds than any other officer in history and got the nickname Cappy. We're not that formal around here...you're Tighe, right! What can I do for you Tighe?"

"Well sir..."

"I'm Cappy."

"Well, Cappy, sir, I'd like to request an assignment change."

"Oh, really, have we done something to upset you? The meal

not to your satisfaction?"

Cappy had a large grin on his face.

"Ah, no sir," Cappy tilted his head sideways, "Cappy, sir," Tighe continued, "I just think I'd be better off with someone other than the partner I've been assigned."

"You and Corinne not get along? Something back at The Point we didn't know about?" FC Dentan continued to smile.

"No sir, Cappy," said Tighe, "She seems very nice, but I think I would do better with, say, one of my outer world mates."

"We don't make that distinction here, son," said Cappy somewhat sternly.

Tighe looked at him with a puzzled expression on his face. "That inner world, outer world crap," said Cappy.

At that moment, Wing Leader Garriger stepped into the room and called out, "How did it go here, Cappy?"

"Well, the briefing went fine, Squints, but sub lieutenant Tighe here, doesn't appear to be satisfied with his ship-mate…asked for a change of assignment."

"Really, the first day! Usually we don't get these requests for the first month or two," exclaimed the Wing Leader in what Tighe thought was an unnecessarily loud voice, "private feud or busted relationship?"

"Um, neither, Ma'am sir."

By now Tighe was ready to run for the doors and disappear into a hole somewhere.

"Prefer to fly a big tub, would you?" asked the Wing Leader.

"No Ma'am, I want to fly a fighter."

Tighe felt he had spoken rather too loudly as well. "Well that's good to hear, because that's exactly what you're going to do," chuckled the Wing Leader, "and you'll be doing the twist with sub-let Corinne Brindar."

Tighe said nothing, just looked confusedly at the Wing Leader. "We call the ship twisters. You'll find out why tomorrow and you will be flying with subby Brindar. Want to know why?"

"Ma'am," responded Tighe.

"Because Brindar and you were far and away the best students and the best flight class jockeys The Point has produced in several years...best students, best flight class Jockey's."

The Squadron leader stepped up to look Tighe directly in the eye. She may have looked small from far away but despite her stature, she seemed plenty big and commanding to Tighe. "That's why we made you and her group leaders, too. Now get out of here and relax. It doesn't get any easier from here,"

Tighe threw a hasty salute and headed for the door. "Oh, and by the way," called the Squadron Leader causing him to stop and turn back, "you can call him Cappy," she said pointing at the Flight Commander, "but don't you ever, ever, call me Squints."

"No Ma'am," and Tighe was out the door and on his way back to his quarters.

When he got back, Corinne was sitting on the bench that separated the doorways of their two rooms. Seeing him, she stood up. "I just wanted to say hi again and let you know I'm ready for you and I to make a great team"

"You know we are the wing leaders," said Tighe, "and we will be doing the twist together and Cappy's ok, but don't call the squadron leader, Squints."

"Thanks for sharing that," responded a bewildered Corinne, "I think I'll turn in now."

"Ok," returned Tighe,

"See you in the morning, mate" said Corinne as she turned

her back, walked to her door and disappeared inside.

"Uh? Oh yeah…mate…"

With that, Tighe couldn't wait another second to get into his room. He threw himself on the bed. "I am an absolute idiot," he groaned pressing his hands against the sides of his head.

It seemed to Tighe as if he had just crawled into bed when he heard the same soft voice that had directed him to last night's briefing say, "Good morning, breakfast is now being served in the Junior officers mess. Follow the yellow lights. Morning briefing will be in your group briefing, debriefing and lecture hall that we will cleverly refer to from now on as BDL"

Tighe was finished dressing just as a knock came at the door. He opened it to see Corinne smiling at him. "Morning mate, since you were right about us being group leaders, I thought it would be a good idea if we went to the mess hall together. You ready?"

Tighe nodded his affirmative and stepped out the door pulling it shut behind him. "Sorry about last night," said Tighe somewhat sheepishly, "I was a bit rattled."

"Well," laughed Corinne, a sound Tighe had to admit he liked very much, "I was a little confused, but I did find out what you meant by doing the twist together. We will be flying a single twister together, it's a small two pilot fighter and pursuit ship officially known as a Deep Space Superiority Fighter which is how its referenced in Government documents and apparently, nowhere else. Everyone else calls it a twister and flying it is called doing the twist. However, I don't quite get the Cappy and Squints stuff."

"Our flight commander wants us to refer to him as Cappy, a nickname he apparently got by forgetting to remove his hat when entering the senior officers mess. It seems you have to buy everyone there a round of drinks every time you do that. He must like the nickname. As for Squints, Cappy called the Wing Leader that. I don't know anything about the reason, but the SL told me in no uncertain terms to never refer to her as that."

"Useful information," said Corinne as they walked into the junior officers' mess hall.

The morning meal while nowhere as elegant and varied as the previous night's banquet, was more than serviceable. As they finished, a single bell rang followed by the same quiet voice that had awakened Tighe earlier, "Please bring your soiled crockery and utensils to the cleaning racks and proceed to your wing BDL." it said.

It was quickly followed by a human voice from behind the cooking enclosure. "That means cups and plates, knives, forks, spoons and chop sticks for those of you who don't know what crockery and utensils mean, and put them on the shelves to your left as you leave."

"Make sure you do," called out another voice. "your mother and her maids aren't here to pick up after you."

As the members of C wing made their way along the yellow pulsating light to the BDL, they were considerably quieter than they had been at breakfast. A pensiveness seemed to emanate from the entire group. Forget yesterday, fun and games were over. They were on their way into battle. It may be a long way down the road, or it may be sooner, but they all knew that was their goal, the place where they were heading and when they crossed the threshold of the BDL hall, their journey to that end would be well under way.

It may as well have been a church rather than a briefing room, so silent were the members of C wing as they took their assigned places. When they were all in place, Flight Commander Dentan along with several others stepped onto the platform that stretched along the front of the room. Dentan stepped to the front edge of the stage while the others sat on the chairs lined up behind him. "I am Flight Commander Dentan, you will call me Cappy, no yessir or nossir, just yes Cappy, no Cappy, whatever you say, Cappy, thank you for saving my ass, Cappy."

A light rumble of laughter swept over the room then quickly ended.

"The officers behind me are the section assessors." continued Cappy, "I will leave it up to them to give you their names when you meet with them right after this. And oh," he added, "if you don't come up with worthy nicknames for your team, that is, your twister, and yourselves, you will be given them. If you wait to be given one, I can guarantee you won't really like it, and I ain't just blowin' rocket juice here."

Cappy paused to let the brief laughter die down then continued, "This is serious business, children, The Vergazan are marshalling for invasion as I speak. We need to be totally ready for them. You and your twister must function like a precise and well-oiled machine. You are the most knowledgeable and best pilots The Point produced this year so we expect nothing but perfection from you, or at least as close to perfection twister teams and twister groups can get. Today is your first day inside the cockpit of a twister. Ok, today, and for the rest of this period, let's call it a week, although it will last approximately ten earth days, you will be learning the ropes on simulators.

Next week, ready or not, you'll be pushing off for simulated drills in your very own twister. I'll tell you and remind you again next week, take care of your Twister. It is not a practice machine, it is yours to love for a very long time. So, keep it safe now and when the Vergazan get here."

After speaking for a few more minutes about care, and discipline and respecting the members of the group because in the end every one's life will depend on it, a set of panels along the walls lit up. Each panel contained a pair of letters from B to Z except for one that said C &CA. To the surprise of the newbies, the seats on which they were sitting, moved in sections each lining up to face one of the panels.

Tighe and Corinne were the first at a number of chairs facing toward the panel bearing the lit up letters C &CA. The woman that came to stand in front of them was not much older than they were. The rank stenciled on the right of the tunic just below the shoulder and on both arms just below the shoulder identified her as having the rank of captain. She informed them that she was a section Captain and they should call her Pookie.

"Actually," she explained, "It was Pukie. I was one of the ones who waited around before choosing a nickname and that's what they gave me. Believe me, there are much worse. Fortunately, I was able to evolve it into Pookie. So, I suggest you don't waste any time coming up with a decent nickname for yourself. My job is to assess your progress as teams. I will be watching and reviewing the simulator results and your first few months during simulated and live weapons drills. I have never had to drop a team and I don't intend to."

Standing up, she added, "follow me and I will bring you to your flight lockers that contain your very own, customized flight suit and help anyone who needs it to put it on."

As it turned out, their flight lockers where in the scramble room adjacent to their assigned quarters. The flight suits were not that different from the training suits they used at The Point

110

except that they were far less bulky. Neither Corinne of Tighe had any trouble putting them on. Pookie then told them to stand in front of their locker holding their helmet under their arm. She stepped in beside Corinne, "Smile for the before picture everyone."

The picture taken, she told the group to follow her to their section simulator room. As she went she pointed to Tighe and Corinne. These are your wing leaders. You may speak informally to me, or Cappy, or any of the section assessors, but all formal details go through them to me or Cappy and then back through them to you. Problems, worries or complaints, they will be filed with Tighe and Corinne and they will pass it on. Cappy will bring it to the executive staff and any response they give will be on paper and given to your group leaders to pass along to you. Your leaders are important members of your group. They didn't particularly earn the position, but you were all examined and they were felt by staff to be best suited to take on this role both on the floor and in the twisters."

They entered an enormous room containing a large number of simulators. Tighe felt pretty good as he and Corinne along with the other teams were led to their particular simulator.

"Our twister is our constant companion. We are expected to get to know it intimately and to love it and we are all completely faithful here, so there won't be a lot of vehicle changes or team changes. You will grow together or you will go together…somewhere else, that is."

Once the group were aboard their simulator and the port closed, Pookie's voice came from somewhere through the curved dash that filled the middle of the cockpit, "Mount your helmets and lock them into the system. Take some time to check out the controls, most are at your fingertips similar to the trainers you operated during your last flight session at The Point. You'll notice that you are to the left of your copilot and facing in opposite directions. Your seating is untethered and free to whatever orientation and attitude you wish, except it won't let you get in the way of your copilot. Your simulator has been designed to be as close as possible to the actual twister you will be running beginning next week."

There was a long pause and then a soft voice much like the one that woke Tighe up filled his helmet. "Phase one, launch sequence and straight and level flight with up to maximum speed will commence in twelve cycles. test controls and seat attitudes before launch,"

Twelve cycles were approximately ten minutes, but for Tighe it seemed like forever. Corinne, too had long since done her testing and seat swinging and there were still four cycles of anticipatory waiting until launch.

"Ships ready for launch on countdown," came the bodiless voice. "Launch to alt-point 7 come to heading 760, maintain heading at alt-point."

There were no real directions in space other than, "that way, or that way, or perhaps, some other way."

While a great deal of effort had gone into developing directional and attitudinal calibration. They tended, however, to be attached to the nearest gravitational body. In combat conditions twister operators would be expected to have developed an innate sense of direction, attitude and speed. Mercifully for the first-time twister the attitude and directional systems were tied to fighter base Charon and that was a good thing because despite the training they got at The Point and their well-honed individual skills when the launch order was given the next few cycles were chaotic.

Twisters smashed into each other and were disabled, others that were able to climb to alt-point seven as ordered could not keep their heading. More twisters collided on the supposedly straight and level. While Corinne and Tighe got to alt-point seven, they did it far more slowly than most of the others who got there, but they quickly lost direction and crashed into another off course vessel. Fortunately for everyone, it happened in a simulator because no team was able to complete the run.

Back in their section in the BDL, Pookie was pretty gentle with them. "That went about the way we expected," she said

That, however was not what the teams expected of themselves and they were angry and wanted to go again. "Look around," Pookie made a sweeping gesture of the other sections. "Notice, they are all here. The simulation," she looked her watch," is still running and everyone is already back. We were far from the first ones. I want you to think about what happened and talk with your team mate. See if you can find out how you can do better. We'll resume tomorrow. Dismissed."

With lots to discuss, the C group made its way back to their flight lockers in the scramble room and then to the recreational area just next door. There, they separated into their team pairs. Tighe and Corinne, like the others racked their brains to try and figure out what had gone wrong. With no real answers forthcoming. Corinne said, "I think I'll work out for a while."

She went to her room and in minutes was back running the indoor track. Tighe watched as others joined her and soon the physical training machines were busy with frustrated fighter pilots punishing themselves for the failure they had never expected. Although the lure to join them was strong, he decided to go back to his room and read up on the twister, the manual that he had found earlier of the desk by his bed. He just couldn't figure out what had gone wrong. Was it his fault? Was it Corinne's fault? Was there something wrong with the simulator. He swore it was not going to happen again. But, it did, the very next day.

They had done a little better on launch and were able to hang around the proper direction. Every time they tried to increase speed, they were thrown off course and once again their simulation ended with a crash.

By weeks end, Corinne and Tighe were able to complete the simulation but had not been able to reach maximum speed so their time was longer than many of the others. The second week was little better. Now they were aboard a real twister. Their particular fighter looked, felt and handled just like the simulator, but their flights were not smooth. They had to work hard to stay on course at speed and when they entered simulated combat their record was one of the poorer ones. Tighe began to detest the buzz sound the twister made when the simulated lasers struck the ship. They survived, but just barely. Had they been in real dog fight, they would be on their way to Repair before too long. Many of the others had gone on to live fire while they spent another week in simulated battle.

While some of the others had their twisters damaged during live fire most were able to handle the course. When Tighe and Corinne went on the live fire course, they somehow squeaked through without getting too severely damaged, but their retaliation fire was spotty at best. Neither Corinne, nor Tighe could figure out what was wrong. Finally, at the end of their first live fire week, Cappy called them to his office.

He sat them down and leaned back on his chair. "I'm very disappointed with your performance. You were touted by The

Point as the best. Your training reports told us you were both gifted fighter pilots, target acquisition was quick and precise, no one could get a bead on you. We agreed. Everything we saw in your records told us that you were destined to be first class fighter pilots. However, the twisters are a different breed of cat. They require two pilots and a great deal of precision and cooperation to master. I suspect you are competing with each other at the controls. Sorry, but that's never going to work. Twisting is not a competition, it requires a relationship between its two pilots that is at least highly cooperative if not symbiotic.

You two are group leaders. You need to be setting the example for the others. I have noticed that your relationship although amicable lacks the closeness, the intimacy, and I'm not talking anything more than an awareness of each other's total personality to be successful. You need to be close friends, at least when you are twisting."

He paused to let that sink in, then dropped the bomb. "If you can't hack it twisting, the ambulance and the supply fleets are looking for good pilots. They say we keep stealing the best pilots away from them. It's probably true. Wouldn't hurt to give some back."

Leaving Cappy's office the two group leaders were devastated. Was Cappy telling them that they were going to be sent to supply or ambulance? "All I've ever wanted was to be a fighter jockey," said Tighe. "I want to fight the Vergazan, not ferry boxes of powdered milk."

"Well, what the hell do you think I want,"

Tighe had never heard Corinne speak so loudly and intensely. "That asshole brother of mine always put me down. Oh yeah, he was going to be a fighter pilot and I was going to make doll dresses. Well to hell with him. I'm a better pilot than he ever dreamed of being. I will not let him get the last laugh. No, I won't."

"I didn't want to say anything," said Tighe, "but I kinda thought your brother was an asshole, too."

For a moment Corinne stared blankly at him and then she started to laugh. "You've met him?"

"Yeah, he told me not to mess with you," grinned Tighe.

"He did! That asshole thinks I can't look after myself?" asked Corinne.

"Guess so," replied Tighe, "He kinda scared the crap out of me."

Corinne roared, "He couldn't fight his way out of a paper bag, and those two friends of his, major duhs. Duh, what now, Garth. Duh, you're so smart, Garth. Duh, your little sister is so cute, duh,what's she doing flying a fighter, duh, duh, duh?"

The two were roaring with laughter as they made their way through the halls back to the junior officers' quarters. As they entered the hallway beside the recreation are, many of the group were staring at them. Tighe looked over then grabbed Corinne around the waist and turned her to look at the gawkers. They began to laugh harder. "Asshole," shouted Corinne at no one in particular and they laughed even harder.

Round and Round, Up and Down

The next few days their twister training didn't show much improvement. They were able to stay on course and hit maximum speed, but their movement were jerky. Inside the twister it was as if they had turned into Alphonse and Gaston an ancient comic routine that had them politely deferring to each other. On those days, they did make all their goals and targets, but it was not done smoothly and as instinctively as it should have been. When Cappy or Pookie listened in on them it was like listening to a kind of Comedy of Manners where formal politeness seemed to be the order of the day, but what really intrigued them was the amount and quality of the laughter it seemed to foster. Whatever was going on Tighe and Corinne were really having fun.

The most interesting thing about the interracial mixture of Lucie and human, most of the Lucie qualities were sublimated and virtually vanished. There were some particularly skilled adepts at telepathy who worked with the Security System, mainly keeping tabs on the Vergazan. The ability to teleport or turn translucent was virtually gone from the now human race. Telepathy consisted of little more than having an inkling in advance that your boss wanted to meet with you in his or her office or that one was about to be called for dinner. To a twenty-first century human, these future humans might seem a bit more intuitive and able to travel further and faster without easily becoming tired.

Sometime, however, between close friends there was a deeper bond. It was an unconscious bond, but made them far more aware of each other and their unspoken needs. This was referred to by Psychologists and Psychiatrist as tapping one's inner Lucie. At some point, Tighe and Corinne tapped into their inner Lucie and the consequence were startling. Overnight their twister missions changed radically.

After many weeks of training during which they not only performed well below expectations, but were on the verge of being withdrawn from fighter command, their performances became slick and skillful. By the end of that last week, they leaped past the others showing incredible agility and the ability to anticipate problems and make corrections at incredibly high speeds. They could change direction in a blink of an eye, taking out target drones before the drones could even direct fire. Command lost so many drones in those last few days that they virtually ran out on the last day of sectional training. In less than a week, Tighe and Corinne had accounted for most of them.

Cappy and Pookie were each certain that in some way they were responsible. Tighe and Corinne were convinced, however, that it was her asshole brother.

With training coming to an end, it was time for everyone to come up with a nickname. They discovered it wasn't that easy. The glamorous ones were all gone. Tighe and Corinne were struggling with their choices and were not very successful. "I don't want anyone giving me a nickname like tiny, or cutie, or something even worse," said Corinne to Tighe as they jogged the recreational room track together.

"Me either," said Tighe, "Oh, hey, back on day one my friend Rodon said that you were a 'freakin' steam zephyr. Why not call yourself zephyr? That's a good one."

"I don't know," said Corinne, "In my mind, I'm more of a breeze than a zephyr."

"Ok, then you're Breeze," laughed Tighe.

Corinne thought about it for a moment. "You know, I won't be able to come up with anything better, myself. Breeze it is. Now we have to come up with something for you."

"Maybe Nitwit or Dumbo," laughed Tighe, "I've often felt that way."

"I think Dumbo's been taken already," said Corinne, "and I can think of a few people that the nickname Nitwit would better serve. You're not that, anyway. You're solid, supportive, sometimes hard to get through to, but ready to block any negativity."

"Sounds like a brick wall," replied Tighe.

"Wally," considered Corinne, "No, but how about Brick. It sounds good."

"Brick it is," laughed Tighe, "Now what about our twister?"

"So, you remember what you would say to me on our way to the scramble room when things weren't going well?" asked Corinne.

Searching his memories and finding nothing, Tighe was forced to say, "Nope, I'm drawing a blank here."

"You said, 'back to the grind'

"I did," Tighe mumbled

" You did, and I think you had already named our twister."

"Grind?" asked Tighe.

"Grind." said Corinne.

Breeze and Brick were ready for the naming session that was part of the informal end of training assembly in the junior officers' mess that evening.

After the congratulation speeches, the toast drinking to each other and a piece of celebratory cake, the naming session began and indeed, most had come up with worthy if not spectacular nicknames. The few who hadn't come up with anything got to listen to the crowd decide what they would be called, nothing really disgusting, but generally not the nicest.

When Tighe and Corinne got up and gave out their nick-names and the moniker of the ship, some wag whose parents were professors of literature specializing in 20th century children saw the B0B-C on the right breast of their fatigues and remembering a title of one of the vast collection of books his parents had gathered, called out, "Breeze and Brick, the Bobbsey Twins."

It became a name they couldn't escape. It was on the front of their tunics it was on their arm patches and it was printed large on the side of their twister, perhaps not Bobbsey, but definitely B0B-C twins.

The next morning each member of the group that had completed training found a package outside their door. It contained two single winged pips, the emblem of a First Lieutenant. They were a pair of shiny new editions ready to join the small sub-lieutenant's pips already neatly packed away. Two sets of newly printed fatigues were delivered not much later. On Corinne's, under the streaming comet, the emblem of twister command was printed, Lt Breeze B0B-C and on Tighe's, Lt Brick B0B-C. This might be a free day, but all the group were out and about having donned their new fatigues to proudly show off their nicknames and their new rank.

As a tribute to the British armed forces of several centuries back, the First Lieutenants were referred to as Lefties, the next rank up were the Looies, after that the rankings were referred to by whether they were sectional, group or divisional Lieutenants. They all meant something, but sometimes even those holding the rank weren't quite sure what exactly the distinction was. They were just grateful for the small increase in pay and the better furloughs the higher-level Lieutenants got.

They had moved from training to practice and the practices got more intense, but the B0B-C twins were more than ready for everything that was thrown at them. In short order, they were promoted through the ranks to group captains. Their weaponry shut down aboard the Grind their role was to play the enemy in dogfights, using laser light to score points on the allied twisters.

Their precision and accuracy and their incredible agility to quickly maneuver into an always successful offensive posture. The B0B-C twins were unbeatable whether facing live fire or laser simulation, they never so much as got a scratch on Grind. What the groups that confronted them did accomplish was a refinement of their own skill, promising a pretty formidable opponent for the Vergazan fighters when the invasion began.

All the training, all the practice, was focused toward the time when the huge Vergazan battle ships with their battle cruiser escorts and thousands of fighters would arrive. The B0B-C group was assigned to escort several space tunnel projector ships, or wormhole carriers as they were more commonly called to the encounter sites. These were the locations where the Vergazan were known to revert to system speeds and materialize to present their intimidating presence to a supposedly unsuspecting humanity.

The Invasion is On

When it finally happened and the long wait was over, the projector carriers were there ready to divert the new arrivals to some place far away, perhaps even to another dimension. Of course, this was not going to happen without a fight. Within a very short time after arriving, a good number of the huge Vergazan Battle ships were gone but a large number of cruisers and countless fighters remained. They amassed around the remaining battleships and especially the Queen ship.

While the element of surprise had been more than successful, the SolSys fighters had very little to do except ward off a few

Vergazan fighters and battle cruisers that were more intent on escaping the carriers and their Space tunnel generators. The very few remaining Vergazan Motherships as well as the Queen ship recognized that their invasion was failing, and ruthlessly ordered a large number of the guardian ships, fighters and battle cruisers to destroy every SolSys vessel they could.

One moment the SolSys ships found their view almost target free the next minute they were facing swarms of Vergazan fighters and a fair number of battle cruisers. There was no subtlety, no fine-tuned strategy in the Vergazan attack. Its goal was to do as much damage to the SolSys ships, carriers, battleships and fighters as possible. The sole strategy seemed to be nothing more than overwhelm with numbers while making little more than a minimum effort to avoid the space tunnel generators and the carriers' disrupters. Seeing this, the SolSys fighter squadrons went into action, the twisters in the vanguard, to meet the suicidal onrush of the Vergazan fighters.

There was an old Earth expression that Corinne suddenly remembered as the B0B-C twins and their group went into a combined defense/attack mode. The expression was about shooting fish in a barrel, something that was supposed to be easy. If the incoming Vergazan maintained the attack deployment they were now showing, destroying them would be like shooting fish in a barrel. The two key things that particular expression doesn't tell one is how many fish there are and how deep the barrel is. "Weird expression," muttered Corinne as she adjusted her balance. "What is?" asked Tighe.

"Old earth expression, 'as easy as shooting fish in a barrel,'" said Corinne.

"Never heard of it," said Tighe. "What does it mean."

"Never heard it in context," responded Corinne, "guess it

meant something at one time."

"Yeah," said Tighe, "but I'm beginning to get a picture."

"Your three," intoned Corinne, and the twister subtlety twisted, there was a brief distortion in space as a disrupter track reached out to one of the lead Vergazan fighters just off to Tighe's right. The Vergazan fighter briefly distorted, then was no longer there..

"Ten high," said Tighe and moments later a Vergazan fighter slightly above the B0B-C's horizontal indicator joined the first fighter in oblivion.

"Grinder low five," echoed a female voice in Corinne and Tighe's headphones.

"On it," they both replied at once, and they were. A third Vergazan fighter ceased to exist.

"Thanks Vente, check your nine." called Corinne.

"Got it, thanks,"

Another voice filtered through Tighe and Corinne's headphones, "Breeze, Brick, watch your flank, there's a small cluster ahead about twenty."

"See 'em, Bronco, let's go," called Corinne.

This internal and external directions continued for some time as the twister, true to their name, twisted and danced among the Vergazan fighters making them appear slow and unmaneuverable. The B0B-C flight and the other twister squadrons continued until leading edge of the Vergazan assault was either dispersed or destroyed.

The twisters were them ordered to withdraw back to their assigned carrier and the sleek, two place Armageddon fighters took their turn. "Nice Job, there, Breezie and Brick," called out Corinne's brother as his Armageddon fighter flashed past Grind.

"Hey, thanks Zapper, thanks Trog, enjoy yourself out there." radioed back Tighe.

"Yahoo," shouted Zapper, who was none other than Corinne's brother, Garth.

"Asshole," she muttered.

While nowhere near as maneuverable as the twister, but with far more firepower the Armageddon ships went to work on the Vergazan fighters. Just as it was with the twisters before them, the Vergazan ships were no match for the Armageddon fighters. Still, the sheer number of the enemy took their toll. No twisters had been lost, but a few had to withdraw for repairs. The Armageddon fighters, in their large numbers in encountering the far larger numbers of Vergazan did take a few losses. The kill ratio favored the Armageddon ships four hundred to one. The overwhelming numbers of Vergazan meant that some would get past the outer group of fighters.

Back with the carriers, the action was not as intense as it was among the Vergazan fighters, but some flanking Vergazan vessels were getting through. In the single mindedness of their attack with the sole intention of destroying the carriers, they were easy targets for the twisters. Those Vergazan that were able to come around the carrier far enough from the wormhole generators in an attempt to flank it almost invariably put themselves into the line of fire of the of the carrier's disrupter cannons. One twister could easily take out any that were remaining. The few Vergazan cruisers not engaged in the defense of the Queen ship did not fare any better.

Never having encountered opposition with the scale and skill of theSol1 System defenses, The Vergazan had never needed to develop anything more than the very basic strategy. It was little more than advance toward the enemy with guns blazing. Many

Vergazan were dazzled by the speed and maneuverability of the SolSys fighters and the quickness and agility of the pilots. They were frustrated that the enemy was hard to hit They broke away from their assault groups to engage a single SolSys fighter in a dogfight. It was invariably a foolish and pointless gesture.

Singley. the Vergazan fighters were no match for the Armageddon fighters or the twisters. Others, confident in their ultimate victory remained with their group and continued to use their excess numbers to try and overwhelm the SolSys fighters. The Armageddon fighters like the twisters earlier were not so easily overwhelmed. They darted among the heavy concentrations of Vergazans, destroying their fighters, seemingly at random, then jump quickly away to regroup.

So, it was a bit of a surprise for Corinne and Tighe to see a Vergazan cruiser stealthily tracking the carrier they were supporting It was staying out of range of the disrupters, while lining up to fire a torpedo-like missile, not at the wormhole generator, or towards its operational center, but at the carrier's tail end.

The Vergazan cruiser's goal was to slow down the carrier and set it up for further attacks. The B0B-C twins and the Grind, immediately set off towards the cruiser prepared to engage. As they approached, the Vergazan deployed several missiles, then turned rapidly away, running a zig zag pattern in an attempt to avoid the twister's guns. "Hey," shouted Tighe, "who is this guy? He's good."

Facing a display of defensive strategy that was totally un-characteristic of most Vergazan, Grind was up to the chase. Tighe and Corinne anticipated the avoidance pattern and were able to hit the cruiser with several laser blasts. While it was clear that they had done some damage to the cruiser, it was still moving quickly and while it did, it changed its avoidance pattern. "Wow," laughed Corinne, "you gotta hand it to the commander of that ship. Pretty damn clever for a Vergazan."

Tighe and Corinne knew that this was not going to be easy, and secretly, they were loving it.

Back at the carrier, the Vergazan missiles had struck, tearing up the rear superstructure and forcing the ship to slow while damage control was put into effect. The call went out to all twisters to return to the ship and keep the hostiles clear while repairs could be done.

Disappointed that they had to abandon this most interesting chase, they turned back. They could see that the Vergazan was heading for a cluster of asteroids. An Armageddon fighter raced past them in hot pursuit of the Vergazan cruiser. "Don't worry," came the voice of Corinne's brother, "We got this."

"Watch yourself, Zapper," said Tighe, "the commander of that ship may be the only Vergazan that knows what to do. If it gets to those asteroids, it'll be tough."

"Will do," replied Zapper.

"No sweat," called out Trog, who was Corinne's brother's team mate, "We got this. This is looking at Vergazan dust in the making."

"Yeah, well be careful," returned Corinne.

Before they had made it back to the carrier, the Armageddon fighter met the Vergazan cruiser at the edge of the asteroid cluster. The result was very different from most SolSys, Vergazan encounters. Seriously damaged, the cruiser was able to slip away among the asteroids. The Armageddon fighter, to Trog and Zapper's surprise, had been hit several times and its propulsion unit was damaged. The two although personally unscathed spent the next few hours sitting out the battle while they waited for the repair ship to come.

The Vergazan cruiser, now severely damaged, left the asteroid cluster in search of a safe place to put down.

Corinne, Tighe and the other members of the B0B-C flight had their hands full back at the disabled carrier. With the Vergazan imperative to get to and destroy the wormhole carriers, a large number of Vergazan fighters had skirted around the fierce, but ultimately futile for them fighter to fighter battle and made their way towards the crippled cruiser. For a short while it was quite intense. Inside Grinder, the direction prompts came fast. "left 3!"

"Right 6!"

"Right 3!"

"2 high!"

"6 low," and so on.

As the number of enemy diminished, Corinne spotted one of the remaining Vergazan perilously close. It was slightly above and to the right of Grind. The controls became hers as she made a seriously risky move, slipping sideways and down to avoid laser tracking by the Vergazan, then spun 180 degrees firing the disrupter as she brought the twister to bear on the rapidly encroaching nose of the Vergazan.

While laser blasts scored Grind's armor shielding, the move was so quick and unexpected that it caused the Vergazan fighter to hesitate, then aim for a broadside. It got within meters before the disrupter had it fully in its sight. The entire heads-up display of the twister filled with an intense flash of bright yellow and red as it passed through the location were moments before the Vergazan fighter, now ash and dust, had been. The screen cleared to show that there were no hostiles near them.

"Give me a high five," shouted Tighe, "I love you."

"Yeah," laughed Corinne, "we'll get married and buy a little cottage with a white picket fence in one of those terraformed asteroids, have a bunch of kids and live happily ever after."

They both roared with laughter. They were SolSys fighter pilots. Their real dream for the future was deep space and reaching out to new star systems and distant galaxies. Still, Tighe wondered why the image of he and Corinne sharing a little house with a white picket fence didn't seem so terrible.

Returning to the carrier, now back under power, they could sense that the battle was coming to a close. The last of the gigantic Vergazan Motherships had been sucked to wherever and the Queen ship was momentarily about to follow. All that remained was to mop up the strays and return to Charon. The Vergazan and their plans to invade earth were finished.

Scattered far from their fellows in distant and unknown regions of the universe, the Vergazan was no longer a threat. They were spread so far and wide that it would be centuries before one Mothership might accidently encounter another assuming they were traveling in the right direction.

Some began colonies, others journeyed on in the vain hope that they would find their way back. Some became space nomads traveling to different worlds to try to keep their ship alive. Others, for whatever reason, fell into suns, or just stopped, lost in space the out of fuel Mothership, now their only home, slowly disintegrating. The threat of the cruel and vicious Vergazan was gone.

Back at Solar System One, its nine planets, and their many communities, the huge space tunnel carriers were being mothballed. They were put away until such time as another threat of invasion might appear. Meanwhile, the fighters and fleet cruisers would search out stray Vergazan, something that would take many earth years.

Modarb Jinglinda Varzzly

In the Vergazan culture, a Modarb could be loosely translated as Princess. Jinglinda was a Princess of the Varrzly clan, a small and ancient branch of the Vergazan royalty. Jinglinda's ancestors had essentially been forced to join the early Vergazan migrations due to the destruction of those early worlds.

Industry on the original home worlds of the Vergazan had polluted and otherwise ruined these home worlds through a ruthless greed. There were few other than the Varrzly who questioned the larger Vergazan society in its ruthless and careless misuse of their home worlds. As their original worlds became uninhabitable the Varrzly and their serfs were forced to join the larger society on its quest for new worlds to make their home.

The bulk of the Vergazan evolved towards the ruthless, destructive beings that discarded worlds, populated or unpopulated after draining them dry of their natural resources then moving on to the next. The Varrzly became more and more the outsider among the Vergazan. It was members of the Varrzly royal family that sat at planning meetings and questioned the wanton destruction. They would have left the main Vergazan body a millennium ago but the destruction of worlds and entire solar systems by the Vergazans was so complete that it would take centuries for them to even be habitable. So they remained, the unheard voice of reason, ostracized and forced to live together on single Mothership at the outer edge of the Vergazan flotilla.

Although over the vast scale of time since leaving their home world many had urged the ouster of the Varrzly clan. Others had even plotted genocide. However, the Varrzly clan had a long and storied history going back before taking to the space between the stars. For most Vergazan, the Varrzly had been with them from the beginning, an annoyance with their talk of peaceful, nondestructive ways, but worthy of staying with the communities, or at least not worth worrying about.

More importantly, the leadership of the various clans were a mean and vengeful lot. They held their position in council of royals with a firm hand. If any single clan, even one as mutually despised as the Varrzly clan were to be exiled or eliminated than any clan could experience the same fate. It was in the best interest of the royal clans that they tolerate the often strange and otherworldly Varrzly clan. The Varrzly's were not fools. They knew it was in the council's best interest to keep them a part of it, pacifist talk or not.

Within their own clan confines, the colossal mother ship and the smaller vessels attached to it, the Varrzly behaved quite different than the others. Propriety and manners were most valued. Communal discussions were frequent for it was through these that the concept of democracy, pacifism and stewardship were kept part of the Varrzly ethos despite the vicious and warlike behavior of all the others.

In battle the Varrzly were the zenith of the Vergazan warriors. They were obliged to join their fellows when a more highly developed people were encountered. Most of these encounters the Vergazan had with other sentient species were pretty straight forward, using their numbers and superior firepower, they quickly overcame the opposition and proceeding on to destroy the planet or the star system and the nearby star systems as well. Countless successful incursions convinced the Vergazan that the simple strategy of overwhelming the opposition worked best.

The leadership of the Vergazan believed their most useful tactic was to terrify and confuse any opposition with and ominous array of large Motherships then quickly beat them down with their advanced weaponry. Along with that, their massive numbers of speedy spaceborne vehicles ready to deal quickly with any opposition was all they felt they would ever need to gain victory over any group in the galaxy . The Varrzly talk of tactics and strategy and special training for fighter and cruiser command and crew was looked upon by the rest of the Vergazans, royal and serf, as foolish, wasteful and absolutely unnecessary.

Among their own, the Varrzly clan encouraged the study of tactics and strategy. They trained their pilots and cruiser crews far differently that the others. They actually would include in their training, variety of attack and defense patterns that made the Varrzly excellent pilots. Members of the clan were often commandeered as trainers for the fighter pilots and cruiser crews of the other clans. They were forbidden from including in their training process any of what the others called the bizarre nonsense they practiced in the Varrzly training procedures. Training the non-Varrzly Vergazan was a pretty simple job for the Varrzly instructors. Their training credo was, 'point your ship, fire your guns and try not to run into each other while you're doing it.'

Modarb Jinglinda was the best pilot and commander the Vergazan had ever produced. She absolutely hated the brutal simplicity of the Vergazan attack. She had honed her proficiency by constantly practicing those bizarre and nonsensical tactical patterns until she knew them cold. Unfortunately for the Vergazan fleet, she was forced to do it on her own and so while procedurally astute, she had never had an opportunity to test it under real or simulated conditions.

Jinglinda was the one who met with the royal council to point out that something was going on among 'The Peoples'' rogue fighters. Somehow their machines had radically increased in both design and battle tactics. While most attributed that success to an accidental technical breakthrough in weaponry, Jinglinda saw much more, how they used cover, how the spaced their attack ships, where the attacks were focused.

The Peoples' rogue defenders had gone from nothing more than armed tugboats to sophisticated pursuit ships that were both fast and maneuverable. She could see that the only thing that assured Vergazan success was The Peoples' fleets limited numbers. The Vergazan greatly outnumbered The Peoples' and The Peoples' ships. while the single-minded viciousness of the Vergazan pilots was brutally focused on annihilating any enemy they might encounter.

Jinglinda suspected that someone was arming and training The Peoples' and that those someones were superior tacticians, capable of at least matching the weaponry of the Vergazan and likely lying in wait somewhere for the Vergazan fleet to come near. She knew that the next goal of the Vergazan was a small solar system in a galaxy across a barren piece of space far from where the Vergazan fleet was being brought to battle readiness.

Although the intel from the distant solar system spoke of a rich group of planets ripe for the picking and a small population in the early days of space flight, Jinglinda found herself distrusting these reports. She had a vague suspicion that while this solar system had a rich group of planets, it might not be so ripe for the picking. Her presentation fell on deaf ears among the council members. Her concerns were limited and speculative. She could provide them with no hard evidence to support her speculations.

Jinglinda commanded a battle cruiser, one that would accompany the Queen ship during the Invasion. She had been removed from her role as senior cruiser commander for the Varrzly Mothership because council did not want her to cause any rift between her clan and all the others. The twenty-eight man crew had been handpicked by Jinglinda from among the best the Varrzly clan had to offer. They were intensely loyal to her, ready to journey into the heart of hell with her if she should ask.

This concerned the council and over the final stages of preparation they had been slowly cycling out the Varrzly crew members and cycling in crew members from the other clans. By the time the Vergazan set out for the distant solar system that housed the planet earth just under half of Jinglinda's original crew members were gone from her ship.

When the ships early on began to run into the warping anomaly, she felt that it was just a little too perfect to be the random effect of space. By then, however, she had learned to keep her mouth shut. She knew she was alone in her doubts and suspicions. Even her clan compatriots dismissed her contentions as pre-battle anxiety. Jinglinda was deeply saddened, knowing that her clan members piloting the cruisers and the fighters, would when ordered, immediately join the massive assault, rushing straight on toward the enemy, guns blazing. If they succeeded, they would be heroes to the fleet, but thoughtless killers to her. If they failed, they would likely be destroyed. Any beings who could withstand and overcome the Vergazan attack would not let any escape.

The moment the invasion fleet crossed the outer reaches of earth's solar system, Jinglinda's worst fears were realized. She saw the carriers and she saw the twisters and she knew that this was a race far more advanced than the Vergazan high council could ever imagine. She could see the forward Motherships being sucked into the great circular windows the carriers bore to disappear completely within moments. When the orders went out for the fighters and escort cruisers to attack the carriers, she saw the twisters race among them, reducing the leading edge of the attack to nothing in very short order, then watched as the Armageddon fighters encountered the Vergazan fighters with nearly the same precision as the magnificently agile smaller ships that had pulled back to guard the carriers.

When she was ordered to join the deployment attempting to destroy the carriers, she immediately obeyed although every fibre of her body and mind told her she and her crew and all the others were primed for extinction.

It was difficult for Jinglinda to control her feelings, feelings that were so terribly contradictory. she found herself admiring the enemy fighters, the way they danced around the Vergazan fighters, making themselves targets that were almost impossible to hit while turning large numbers of Vergazan fighters to trash and ash. They were magnificent. She also felt a sadness that her people, including her own clan members were being decimated.

As she approached one of the large carriers, she watched the Vergazan fighters wasteful forward attack being easily turned away by those magnificent little gyrating fighters. Those few others that tried to flank the carrier beyond disrupter range were either sucked into the mysterious window or ran straight into the carrier's battery of disrupters as they closed.

Feeling the need to at least show some support for her people, Jinglinda began to work her way around the carrier. She saw the far-side battery of disrupters and the laser turrets and was able to set up an attack pattern that would eventually bring her into fairly close quarters with the carrier and inflict some serious damage or even destroy it. While the forward crew armed and loaded the torpedoes, she detected, over the top edge of the carriers that one of the small gyro fighters had spotted her. Its wheeling attack would momentarily have her ship within range. She had no choice but to move off from the larger vessel or either the carrier's disrupters or the fighters would end any hope she had of successfully terminating it. Her second in command, one of the council's planted crew members, screamed at her. He tried to wrest control of the ship from her. "Get in there, take it out, " he shouted, "or I will!"

One of Jinglinda's loyal clansman who was on the bridge, grabbed him before the second in command could pull her from the controls. She drew off from the carrier and let it pass as she did, she brought her cruiser in behind the carrier. She was taking laser fire from the small fighter and knew that she would shortly be in range of its disrupters. As she ordered the first torpedo to be released, a disrupter, fortunately still at maximum range, had done some damage to her cruiser's outer armor. Already plotting an escape pattern, she released two more torpedoes.

As she made her escape towards a distant asteroid cluster where she hoped she could hide, she could see in her displays flashes on the rear surfaces of the carrier and that annoying and deadly fighter fast on her tail. Jinglinda knew she had done some damage to the carrier. She didn't know it was the first and only serious damage any of the SolSys carrier ships would experience.

She could tell the fighter on her tail was figuring out her escape pattern and was doing some damage with its long range lasers. Immediately she changed her pattern. She watched wonderingly as the fighter began to fall back and out of range. Was it out of fuel, unlikely.

She felt a moment of satisfaction, it was being recalled to protect the carrier. She must have done some serious damage. Jinglinda had no more than a few seconds to enjoy that thought when she detected a second ship speeding past the withdrawing fighter. It was one of those slightly larger and just as deadly fighters. It may not handle as well as the smaller fighter, but could outrun her damaged cruiser. She began calling out orders to the gunnery crew while she continued to vary her escape pattern. The asteroid cluster was closer now. She had to make it. She called to her gunnery crews to set their weapons at a particular set of coordinates and had them hold their fire. The more restless among the council's plants manning one set of weapons, a laser-like cannon began shooting, it was poorly directed and missed the fighter completely. Jinglinda's clansmen held their fire as ordered. The cruiser made a quick quarter turn and Jinglinda yelled fire.

Flames blossomed from the side of the attacking fighter, but were quickly extinguished. She knew the fighter was damaged, but it had some capabilities remaining. Long range lasers swept across the cruiser's back end. Between that last laser sweep and earlier damage from the other fighter Jinglinda was not surprised when the condition reports started coming in. They had been fatally damaged. As she slipped among the asteroids, Jinglinda ordered the repair crew, basically anyone still alive and mobile, to do everything they could to keep the cruiser going. Their ship would no longer be viable in a combat situation, but just might bring them somewhere where they could safely put down.

Bringing her crippled battle cruiser to the edge of the asteroid cluster, Jinglinda scanned for both enemy ships and a possible safe refuge. There were no enemy fighters to be seen, but there was a large gas giant not too distant that promised a moon where she could bring the cruiser to ground and possibly attempt repairs. There was little choice, between the loss of atmospheric gases and the exposed construction materials leaking toxic vapors that would eventually fill the cruiser. She and her crew would die a painful death within a fairly short period of time. Their only hope was to find a satellite off the nearest gas giant planet. She began the long journey to the distant planet, her ship limping along at a severely reduced speed.

12

The Soshen of Titania

Except for the military bases and their civilian holdings on Pluto and Charon, Titania, the largest of Uranus' moons along with Titan was among the most distance from the sun to be terraformed and settled. It was, in fact, only partly terraformed a large lake had formed creating what appeared to be a wide fresh water river around what was, with the solar tunnel, the equator.

The terraformed region of Titania was a several hundred mile expense, primarily of cooperative farms on each side of the equatorial lake. These farms belonged to a communal cult called the Soshen. Their name was a derivative of the ancient Irish word for peaceful. No one is sure how it got its name. It had originally formed on earth around the time that the terraforming of Mars and the asteroids had begun.

It was a group that combined the Lucie and the human desire for a life of work and peace. The cult was completely pacifistic and when the invasion threat from the Vergazan had become a reality, the members had moved to Titania establishing it as an agricultural planet. The early arrivals had seeded the lake with fish and by the time of the invasion battle, although relatively small, was a key link in the solar system's agriculture. Its fish were renowned for their size and unique edibility and while most Soshen communities focused on farming, there were a number of communities devoted to the fishery industry catching, packing and shipping high quality fish products throughout the system communities.

It was also a favorite spot for wealthy anglers and company executives using angling as part of their team building. A number of fishing outposts and a large sized town had added a secular aspect to the community.

Since it was a specialized tourist hotspot reachable in minutes via wormhole passages from every major center throughout the system, Titania's peaceful community found itself compromised by minor criminal activity. A highly trained security force was established to maintain the peace, particularly in the central town that was quickly growing to city dimensions and in the large and fancy lakeside compounds that belied the name fishing outposts.

As the threat of war grew, and with it the possibility that Vergazan might send forces to invade the outer communities, SolSys Marines were dispatched to the outlying colonies. Titania was now well protected from the enemy by its own security forces and the detachment of highly trained and well-armed Marines assigned there.

Jinglinda and her crew knew nothing of this as they made their way to the nearest planetoid that appeared to offer safe refuge. That planetoid was, in fact, Titania. Jinglinda's cruiser was approaching one of the unterraformed polar regions. Damaged long range sensors were unable to pick out the settlements. Even if they had been able to detect the signs of humanity, the cruiser would have had to make for it none the less as the damage was reaching the critical point. Titania was Jinglinda's only option.

Jinglinda and her crew didn't see the settlement and the settlement didn't see them. She approached the polar region of Titania with a plan to ease the cruiser down on the smoothest bit of earth she could find. As she made her final approach, she let the moon turn under her. That is when a moment of mutual recognition occurred. Jinglinda saw the settlement and the security forces and the Marines saw Jinglinda. Being airborne, she still had the advantage. At least she had enough advantage to change direction and bring her cruiser down at the edge of the polar waste just beyond the terraformed land.

The land may not have been terraformed where she chose to land, but readouts on her close range sensors informed her that there was an atmosphere and although it might not be exactly to her liking, was close enough for survival. This was a good thing as far as she and the crew were concerned as the twisting metal sounds they heard on forced landing was the ship readying itself for the scrap pile. Under Jinglinda's steady hand, the ship didn't break up or roll.

Before it came to a full stop, crewmembers were at the weapons locker, grabbing whatever they could.

Jinglinda left through the forward airlock along with twenty-three of her crew members. While her faithful clansmen among the crew gathered around her, the others gathered around her second in command. Jinglinda turned to face him. "What are your plans, sub-commander?" she asked.

Before the sub-commander could articulate his message, two marine drop ships and a Security launch screamed overhead. Armored Marines were nearly on the ground as he responded, "fight the enemy with everything we have."

The sub-commander and his followers dove into the rock piles, seeking to shelter their attack on the arriving Solsys Marines. Jinglinda dropped her weapon to the ground and signaled her followers to do the same. Some more than others reluctantly put their guns down and continued to stand with her, one eye on her and one on the approaching Marines.

The sub-commander and his group opened fire. The Marines, however were trained for this and quickly took cover. Within moments seven of the sub-commander's group were dead. Three others, including the sub-commander had taken advantage of the brief fire fight to attempt an escape among the huge boulders and large rocks. Several Marines broke off to follow them. The remainder approached Jinglinda and her loyal crew members. One of the lead Marines held something that looked like an earphone towards Jinglinda and in the squeaky, subsonic tones of Vergazan speech said, " take this!"

The accent although not quite the formal language of the Varrzly, wasn't bad thought Jinglinda as she shrugged and reached for the mechanism he proffered. These beings had obviously anticipated the Vergazan long before the invasion attempt to have been able to learn even a few words in Vergazan.

Holding the earpiece as the one handing it to her modelled by putting his hand to his ear, she was surprised to find that she could understand his speech without difficulty. "I am Major Davrick, commander of the thirty-seventh Marine Detachment, Sol One, Solar system Defense. You are our prisoners."

"Commander Jinglinda Varrzly, Varrzly clan, Vergazan. That

is the remains of my ship behind you. I ask quarter for my crew, at least the ones who stand with me.",

The Solar system Marines might look soft within their artificial carapaces, but Jinglinda knew that they were not to be taken lightly. "Thank you, commander," said the one called major, "so long as your people are co-operative we will protect you from harm," and he raised his hand to his forehead in what Jinglinda recognized as a salute.

She returned his salute with the Varrzly clan salute, two hands crossed palms open towards the other.

Although she had every reason to expect these beings to treat her and her crew brutally for that is how the Vergazan would treat their prisoners, she was surprised at their restraint. Their weapons were trained on herself and the crew, but they were disciplined and amazingly respectful as she and her loyal crew was directed to the now grounded security system launch.

The seats aboard the launch were passable. Some of her taller confreres would have sore joints by the time they got to where they would be taken out and imprisoned.

To the humans the Vergazan looked gangly and awkward. They could not tell immediately if their armor was a natural outgrowth or something they put on when going to battle. The major and his men weren't sure of the exact nature of the creatures they were escorting. They showed hints of reptilian as well as insectile ancestry.

They were amazed by the placid behavior of the crew members as they marched into the lock up behind their poised commander. This behavior was not what the humans saw as typical of the Vergazan. Most, according to the communications messages had continued to fight with a single-minded and self-destructive fury well after it was clear the battle was over.

While some might have gone into hiding, most were destroyed in suicidal attacks against what they must have by then known to be a far superior fighting force. None had showed the calmness in surrender that these twelve Vergazan did. All down the line right to the senior planning committee back on Mars, the news of the small group of Vergazan that had surrendered was making noise.

Questions flew fast and furious. Was this some kind of secret cabal that was about to suddenly rise up and wreak destruction? Where they planning something terrible? Did they have some kind of secret contact with their fellows and were sending them intelligence about the solar system and the humans? Or, were they some kind of pacifists? They did crew a battle cruiser that had clearly been in action.

Curious members of the Soshan joined the others at the prison compound. The others may have seen them as vicious enemy, but the Soshan weren't sure. They sensed a dignity and discipline among these odd and alien creatures. The could see the respect they held for the one who had identified herself as the commander of the Vergazan battle cruiser.

While the prisoners were being prepared to be sent to Solsys headquarters for examination and questioning. The Soshan leaders asked if they could talk to one of them, preferably the one who was the commander. At first the military were inclined to forbid this, but Soshan were important members of the Titanian community. The leadership back on Mars felt there was little harm in allowing the meeting, and they might learn something they wouldn't otherwise garner. The prisoners would be leaving Titania shortly, so they decided to give the Soshan a few minutes with Jinglinda and one of her crew.

When the Soshan interviewed Jinglinda, she explained to them how her clan was different from the other Vergazan clans. How they stressed respect and self-discipline. She explained how her clan came to be with the larger body of Vergazan and why they felt constrained to participate in their invasions. They kept mainly to themselves otherwise, focusing on education and gentility.

When they spoke with one of Jinglinda's lesser clansperson, it confirmed for the Soshen that they were exactly what they claimed to be. As the Transfer Team arrived to take Jolinda and her fellows to the vehicle that would bring them through the wormhole to SolSys headquarters on Mars, the Soshen were able to express to Jinglinda a decision they had made in short council after the interviews. They informed Jinglinda and the commander of the Transfer Team that should the central control agree, the Vergazan of the Varrzly clan would be provided homesteads on Titania. This offer was with the proviso that they adhere to the principles of the Soshen and eventually become part of the Soshen union.

The SolSys committee made a lengthy and careful evaluation of the risk factor of the small group of captured Vergazan. At one point Jinglinda had asked about the wormhole generators that had swallowed the Vergazan mother ships. She was happy to hear that her people had not been intentionally destroyed, but rather had been sent off to the far reaches of the universe. She told the committee that in doing so, they may well have done a great favor for Varrzly allowing them to find their way free from their barbarian cousins.

The committee found Jinglinda and her retinue not to be a threat, and they were returned to Titania where with the help of the Soshen they were able to set up several homesteads. The

Varrzly Vergazan retitled themselves the Varrzly Perganzan which meant "peaceful and productive Varrzly. They proved to be excellent at agriculture and as members of Soshen. Their tiny community flourished. Within a generation they were granted full Sol One System citizenship. They became good friends and neighbors too ,

Some of The Peoples' whose home worlds were too badly damaged to hold large populations emigrated to the Sol One system and along with the Varrzly Perganzan became loyal citizens. The Sol One system was soon verging on becoming a co-operative and productive multi-species society.

Despite the Vergazan attempt at invasion and conquest being foiled, the system that housed earth, now called home world, was undergoing change. Terraforming continued to the point that every sizeable asteroid and planetary satellites would eventually be habitable. Neighboring star systems offered potential for expansion. A new age of exploration was about to get underway.

13

The Three Musketeers

Thanks to their combined earth human and Lucie human heritage, Corinne and Tighe remained as living pieces of history. The twisters were long since mothballed against a time they might be called on again to run shotgun for SolSys One. Their technology constantly updated, they were not merely fossils waiting for a last run, but evolving war machines with no wars projected. Should there ever be a need, however, they would be more than ready. That is, except for Corrine and Tighe's ship The Grind B0B-C. It was housed in the Smithsonian. Hanging in a pseudo combat pose in the Hall of Victory, A chamber dedicated to the Vergazan Invasion. The chamber located on Mars boasted a most advanced wormhole technology.

Entering the Chamber whether from the Washingtonian main building or the Barsoomian Annex, was nothing more than stepping through a wide doorway. If you so chose, as many young people did, you could comfortably stand at the threshold with one foot on earth and one foot on Mars

Corinne and Tighe, although living pieces of history were,

fortunately not required to hang around in the Hall of Victory. They were well represented by 3D images and pseudo replicants. As Tighe more than once said, "Doesn't seem to matter where I am in that gigantic room, I keep running into myself. I wouldn't mind if he didn't always look so much younger than me."

Age, rank and hero status has its privileges so Corinne and Tighe were able to be on stage to attend the graduation of their great grandson from The Point where they had met so many years before. Their great granddaughter had graduated a year earlier and was now doing space lane security among the inner planets. She had already risen to the rank of Lieutenant and they were enormously proud of her They felt the same pride for their grandson, but because they had advanced knowledge of his placement were intrigued and excited for him. He was to be assigned to a newly formed Deep Space Corps, Explore and Outreach Division, the Trail Blazers.

Not very far away from the stage Modarb Anderra Varzzly Granddaughter of Modarb Jinglinda Varzzly, the title having become an honorific for the eldest female of the generation and her sire. They were there to celebrate the graduation of their oldest daughter from The Point. This was the first graduation class of SolSys Security to include the newest citizens the Varrzly Perganzan and The Peoples'. There was, in fact, a good-sized cadre of Perganzan and The Peoples'

The newest citizens as they were referred to, had proved themselves well deserving of citizenship and of participation in the SolSys Security. What the proud parents and relatives did not yet know, the best of the graduates representing all three SolSys species would be assigned to the Trail Blazers. Each five man ship would have at least one of The Peoples' and a Perganzan along with a human.

Over four years at The Point great friendships were formed. One of the best trio of friends was called the Three Musketeers by their classmates. Where that name came from, no one was sure, somebody at The Point must have been reading up on pre-Lucie earth. Anyway, it seemed to work and work well. They were inseparable. They worked together, studied together and had each other's backs socially and shipboard. Darak, Great grandson of Corinne and Tighe was never found too far from his best buddies, Anderra of the Perganzan and Sybent of 'The Peoples'.

After the extended training on the deep-space Trail Blazers through a miracle, or perhaps many hours of discussion at command, the Three Musketeers, each of whom would have made a worthy commander of their own ship were assigned together to the same ship. Joining them were other close Point classmates, Anarina and Sandiria a human and a People's female. Both top of their class in diplomacy and one on one combat.

To Anarina and Sandiria's delight, it was the Three Musketeers who were made the face of the Explore and Outreach Division. The two were more than happy to stay in the background while the Musketeers spent the months before their two year stint into the uncharted regions of distant space in front of the holocams.

In the months before they left, the Three Musketeers became not only the face of the Explore and Outreach Division of SolSys, but the face of the future. Their collective image was everywhere. They were on posters, in holograph advertisements, on billboards, three young heroes, the vary image of resolute pride and strength with a far off look in their eyes.

The holocams were there in numbers as they boarded the specially designed reinforced long range ship It was a beauty with its reserve fuel containers and launching from Mars base, it cut a gallant figure as it slowly rose through the atmosphere until it became a pinpoint far off in the darkness of inter planetary space. The slow grace of the launch was purely symbolic as it could have gone into hyperjump within a second of leaving the launch cradle.

The Three Musketeers and their fellow crew members where the first of thirty Trail Blazers to be launched over the next few days. Each manned with a highly capable, well trained multi-species crew ready, as with the ancient saying, "to boldly go where no one had gone before."

Before moving from Explore and Outreach to SolSys Command, Darak, Anderra and Sybent eternally labelled the Three Musketeers in the history books, had completed one two year mission and several five year missions. During that time, they had discovered many empty worlds ready for terraforming and settlement. They had also made a number of first contacts. Most of the intelligent species they encountered were relatively primitive as far as their technology. Some were more socially advanced than others and a few were on the brink of entering their own space age.

For those ready for the encounter with the highly advanced SolSys civilization they joined in a loosely structured alliance that assured them a level of safety and continued development. These alliances, as there were a modest number of societies at that stage of development the Trail Blazers, had encountered would eventually form a federation of allied worlds. It provided peace, security, and assisted development throughout the galaxy and beyond that would last for several millennia, perhaps even much longer.

There would be no more invasions for the foreseeable future. Earth and its solar system, the Sol One System had experienced two invasions, one that proved highly beneficial and one that was successfully foiled. Those would be the only ones. The history books extolled the luck of the earth based community. For the most part they delighted in this image of luck, but even the majority of citizens, historians included had no idea just how lucky earth and its system communities really was.

Two years into their second mission, the first five year one, the Three Musketeers and their crew came across a vast field of space wreckage. Investigations proved it to be the site of an enormous battle to the death of two separate species. The remains they found in the wreckage of the gigantic ships were unlike any species they would ever come across in the remainder of their travels.

The ships of each of the two species represented in the scene of mass destruction were found to have early radio transmissions from the beginnings of the age of technology on earth. Hyperjump co-ordinates to the source of these transmissions had been entered into the drive modules of both sets of ships. The open area of space, now cluttered with the wreckage of two gigantic fleets was an excellent marshalling region for an invasion fleet to amass before hyperjumping to earth's co-ordinates.

Although they would never know for certain what had occurred, the crew of the Three Musketeers' Trail Blazer could speculate with some certainty. It would seem that two invasion fleets from different parts of the galaxy or beyond, enroute to invade a helpless earth had somehow arrived at the same location and time to mount their invasion. Neither side was prepared to forfeit their potential claim and battle ensued. Here in this region of space, far from any solar system, the battle raged until no ship on either side remained to even find a refuge among the stars.

The utter brutality of this encounter was testimony to the ruthless nature of both invasion forces. Had either fleet successfully reached earth, that tiny world and its future as Sol1Sys would never have been achieved. Had they not met in this empty piece of space, one or two species prepared for ruthless conquest as destructive as the Vergazan might still be trashing worlds. Most members of the Sol1System and the members of the federated alliance of worlds would never know just how truly lucky they all were.

www.ingramcontent.com/pod-product-compliance
Lightning Source LLC
Chambersburg PA
CBHW050952120626
46552CB00001B/499